The Secret Life of the D

B

Jeannie Ruth

To
Jessie —

We all have our little

Secrets —

Jeannie Ruth

Author's Note

I want to remind my readers that I like fact with my fiction. Therefore, I make the background for my stories as realistic as possible. The Story takes place in the mid 1700's. The Andros family was a very important part of the history of the Channel Islands and smuggling was a very important part of that history. John Ayscough was the interim governor of Jamaica during this time period and the problems on the island are quite real. All the information about the areas mentioned in this book are true. Except for the afore mentioned people, the characters are strictly from my imagination.

Chapter One: The Problem

Two o'clock in the afternoon, Jamison entered the servant's work room and looked around. He saw Riggs sitting at the table, polishing a pair of His Grace's boots. He approached him and held out the card in his hand. "This gentleman says he has urgent business with His Grace. He will not take no for an answer."

Riggs did not look up from his work. "His Grace's orders are that he is indisposed and is not seeing visitors."

Jamison looked uncomfortable, shoved the card so Riggs had no choice but to read it and said, "He says if His Grace will not come to him, he will go to His Grace. I do not see how we can tell him 'no'."

Riggs looked up and raised an eyebrow as he read the name. He frowned and shook his head. "I am quite sure His Grace will be unable to see anyone."

Jamison glared at him. "Fine, then you can go tell Lord Peters to leave."

Riggs sighed. "Very well," he said rising. "I shall go see His Grace. I'll do my best, but in his condition, I'm not sure what I can do."

Riggs entered His Grace's bedroom from the servant's entrance. He sighed. His Grace always insisted his valet not wait up for him. He was a kind man that way. In his youth, he had been extremely late many a time. Then after his marriage, he slept with his wife most every night, not wishing his valet's presence as they readied for bed. Now, sadly, there were nights that ended up like this.

This afternoon Riggs found His Grace in a deplorable state. He had managed to divest himself of his evening coat and waistcoat and shoes, but not out of his shirt and breeches. He was sprawled across the bed uncovered. The maids always turned back the coverlet and sheets for him, but last night he hadn't found his way into the bed.

Riggs stood at the end of the bed and said in a not too loud, but clear voice, "Excuse me, Your Grace, but Lord Peters is here, and he insists on seeing you at once."

There was no response.

Riggs moved to the side of the bed and leaned in closer and said a little louder, "I am sorry, Your Grace, but Lord Peters is most insistent. Please, Your Grace, he will come to you if you can't come to him. I really think you would not like that."

Again, no response.

Riggs sighed and quietly arranged His Grace in a proper sleeping position and covered him with the sheet and coverlet. Riggs desperately tried one more time. "Your Grace, please wake up." No movement. He signed and laid the card on the bedside table and slowly went down to try and convince their guest to wait until another day.

Chapter Two: The Proposition

Vincent Pomeroy, Duke of Edgingham, slowly became aware that someone was shaking his shoulder. He started to stretch, but the movement caused his stomach to rebel. His head was throbbing, and he desperately needed to relieve himself; but as he opened his eyes, he closed them again, because when he did, the room dipped and swirled. "Riggs, why are you waking me up so early?"

He heard a familiar voice, but not Riggs say, "I asked your valet to give us a few minutes. He should be here shortly, and it is past three in the afternoon. I do not call that 'early'."

His eyes flew open and he slowly, very slowly turned his head toward the voice. It took a moment for his vision to clear and he saw his old friend standing by the bed. "Simon, what are you doing here?"

"I have urgent business with you, but you were too indisposed to come downstairs, so I came up to you." At that moment Riggs entered. "I will leave you with your valet, but if you are not downstairs in the library in one hour, I will be back." He turned and left the room.

Nearly an hour and several cups of strong tea later, Vincent was bathed, dressed and mostly sober. Riggs stayed quite near him on the stairs as he descended a little unsteadily to the first floor. Once they had made it safely to the library door, Vincent took a deep breath and said, "Thank you Riggs, I shall be fine from here." Riggs returned to His Grace's chambers to straighten up the rooms and prepare clothes for the day.

Vincent took a few slow breaths and opened the library door. He forced a smile as he entered. Simon rose and approached his friend. "Simon, old friend," Vincent said, shaking his hand. "Tis good to see you. I will ring for tea. Can you stay for dinner?"

"I already took the liberty of ordering a substantial tea, I thought you needed something to eat. I am sure your cook knows what you like."

Vincent moved to his favorite chair, motioned for his friend to take the one across from him and they both sat. "Yes, Mrs. Bailey does. Thank you." He hesitated. "You said you had urgent business. I cannot imagine what could concern me. I have retired here to the country."

"I know. We have been friends a long time, so I will be blunt and come to the point. I cannot stand seeing you drink yourself to death like this. Andrea would not have approved, and you know it. You need to find some project to keep you occupied and

I have just the thing. The Home Office has some delicate matters that need attending to, and well, to be brutally honest, your current condition makes you a perfect choice."

Vincent opened his mouth to reply, but there was a knock at the door. "Enter," he called. It opened and Jamison entered, followed by a footman carrying a large tray. Jamison began setting up tea on the low table in front of the chairs in which he and Simon were sitting. "That will be fine," commented Vincent as he was finishing. "We can take care of ourselves, but please see that we are not disturbed. Oh, and tell Mrs. Bailey we have a guest for dinner."

"Yes, Your Grace," replied Jamison as he and the footman left the room. After shutting the door, Jamison said to the footman, "Davis, give me that tray and you station yourself here across from that door and allow no one in the area until His Grace leaves the room or tells you otherwise."

Davis replied with a grin, "Aye, aye, Mr. Jamison." He got a sharp look from the butler. He wiped the smile off his face and replied, "Yes, Mr. Jamison."

Simon immediately began loading a plate with the little sandwiches. "I hope you do not mind if I dive in. I am quite starved."

Vincent laughed. "You always enjoyed good food and my cook is excellent." He helped himself to a small sandwich. "You must spend the night, tis too late to get back to London tonight."

"I had planned to spend the night. We have much to discuss."

Vincent sighed. "I shall listen, but I am not interested in politics these days."

"Politics does not really have anything to do with it. I know once I could trust your secrecy; but can I still?"

"Of course. Whether I am interested in it or not, I would not tell a soul. Besides, I do not have guests, there is no one to tell."

"These will be special assignments, secret missions if you will. Things that the Home Office cannot officially do anything about. No one will know about them but you, and me, and the Secretary. You may pick your own men, do what you will to solve the issue. You distinguished yourself in the Navy before you inherited. You know how to handle things. You would be on your own. Most could be dangerous. We need someone we can trust implicitly." Simon finished his sandwiches and helped himself to scones with jam and clotted cream.

Vincent sighed. "I am really not interested in getting involved in anything. I am quite content to stay in the country and ..."

"Drink yourself to death!" interrupted his friend. "Andrea would be furious. She would not want her death to end your life as well. You were spared from that tragedy for a reason. And what about Alistair? Do you think he wants to have to come home and take over your estates, when he is having a marvelous time in Jamaica? Stop being selfish, man, and use the life God gave you for a good reason! Your country needs you. Do the right thing."

"I have gone too far down that road. I do not think I can turn back."

"Yes, you can. But do not go too far. You being a known sot is a good cover. No one would suspect you doing undercover work for the Crown. Get yourself together, but do not let anyone know. Use it to your advantage."

Vincent was considering what had been said. "Because you are my friend, I will give it every consideration; but let us talk of other things for awhile. Give me time to think. I cannot wrap my head around all this right now."

Simon nodded. "Till after dinner then." Then he changed the subject to other more mundane topics. Simon kept the conversation on London gossip and news, throwing in a few things he thought might be useful to bring Vincent up to date.

After they finished their tea, Vincent excused himself. "I regret I must leave you until dinner. I have some business affairs that need my attention. You might like to see the garden which is out those glass doors," he said pointing to them. "Please feel free to make yourself at home. Tell Jamison if you desire anything. I will see you in the Drawing Room at eight."

At that he went to his office and out his private exit, so he could leave unseen. He hurried away from the house into the orchard and found his favorite spot for contemplation. He smiled as he sat on the bench that he had placed under the huge apple tree. The orchard was full of apple, pear, and plum trees, but this was the largest of them. It had been here the longest, survived all sorts of things. It was because of this tree he had met Andrea; but he would not think of that right now. His life had changed under this tree, if it was to change again, this was the place to consider that. He sighed as he sat down. "I am five and forty years of age. Do I really want something so adventurous?" He spent the next couple hours in thinking about Simon's proposal. It was not a proposition to be taken lightly. It had been rolling around in his mind since Simon brought it up, but now he took some time to really concentrate on it. He smiled when he heard the gong signaling time to dress for dinner. It was not usually rung outside, but Jamison had not found him in the house and knew where he was.

Chapter Three: The Decision

He met his friend promptly at eight in the Drawing Room. Dinner was announced shortly thereafter. "My cook serves à la française when it is just me, so I hope you don't mind."

"Not at all. We do it that way as well when dining en famille. I, and my family, find being served one dish at a time rather tedious. I like it all on the table so I can decide what I want and what I do not," replied Simon.

Mrs. Bailey usually set a fine table for His Grace and despite having company on short notice, she had outdone herself. There was Pease Soup, Roast Duck with a Red Wine Sauce, Boiled Cauliflower, Dressed Broccoli, Steak and Kidney Pie, Venison with Roasted Mushrooms, with Gateau de Pomme, and Syllabub for dessert. Vincent enjoyed watching Simon eat until he was quite stuffed. Vincent had to force himself to taste the different dishes, his stomach was still not ready for much.

Finally, Vincent asked, "Shall we retire to my study for our Port and cigars? We can talk quite privately there." Simon nodded and followed his host out of the room.

Once they were behind closed doors, Vincent said, "Simon, you are a really good friend and I know that we both speak in confidence. Due to what you are asking, I need you to understand that I am not a total drunkard. I let myself get lost in the bottle too often, yes; but I can leave it alone as well. I wanted that drunken image to get out, as it makes people leave me alone. Otherwise, everyone feels sorry for me and feels they must keep me occupied. I prefer to keep my own company. So you need not worry that I will blow a mission. That being said, I will listen to your proposition. I still reserve the right to bow out if I do not like your details."

"Good enough. I know you well, Vincent. I would trust you stone cold sober or falling down drunk or I would not have asked you to do this."

"Very well, go ahead, what do you need of me?"

It was quite late or rather early in the morning when they finally called it a night. "I will give you a definite answer at breakfast, if that is agreeable. I am interested in your offer. I just have a few things I need to decide upon."

"Quite understandable. I know I am asking quite a lot."

Vincent nodded. "And just so we are clear, I will answer only to you and the Secretary?"

"You will not really have to answer to anyone. We will only send you things that need to be handled. The decisions on whether you want to do the mission or not and how to handle things will be yours. The Bank of England will handle all monetary issues as it always does. I know you handle your finances there. You can recruit whomever you like to assist you. However, if you get into trouble, there will be no one to bail you out, therefore you can always say no. I know what I am asking, but I trust you implicitly. I bid you good night. What time is breakfast?"

"Since it is just me, breakfast is whenever I want it. I am sure you are anxious to return to London. Shall we say seven?"

"That is quite agreeable." Simon left the room. Vincent thought for just a few more minutes, then nodded his head and rang for Davis.

When Davis arrived, Vincent did not give him time to speak. "I am sorry for the late hour, but I need to see you, Jamison and Riggs in my chambers as soon as you can all assemble, and please tell Mrs. Bailey that Lord Peters and I need breakfast at seven. He will be leaving after that."

Davis nodded, "At once, Your Grace," and left the room.

Vincent went upstairs. He had already divested himself of his coat and waistcoat when they arrived. "Well, men, we have been together a long time. Our life has been rather quiet here in the country.

That may be about to change. I know I can trust you all implicitly. I have been asked to do something that could be dangerous. If you desire to continue working here, it will inevitably include you one way or another. I understand if you want no part. We are all no longer young bucks. If you desire to continue to lead quiet lives, I will give you excellent references and help you find work elsewhere and you may leave. If you stay, you are committed to be involved at some level. Before I can expound on that, I need to know if you are with me?"

The three men all looked at each other and nodded. Riggs replied immediately, "I have been with you since I was assigned to you aboard the Bertrand. When you left the Navy, you promised me a place. I am honored to still serve you. I am with you all the way."

Davis added, "When I were pressed into service, I was very young. I fought it. You helped me, gave me a chance. You offered me a place when you left. I am with you now no matter where you go."

Jamison spoke up, "Then I can safely say, we are all with you, Your Grace. We may not all be young or as spry as we used to be, but our minds and our hearts are still strong. We are with you, Your Grace."

"Excellent, I really prefer your involvement. Please, pull up a seat." He remained standing and did some pacing while he talked. He proceeded to explain his conversation with Lord Peters. When he finished, he stopped pacing and turned to look at the men.

"Riggs, you have been so much more than my valet. You have been my aide, spy, associate, friend for many years. I hope you will continue to be at my side as we do this?"

"Most assuredly, Your Grace. I would not miss it. I am ready for more excitement in my life." Riggs said with a grin.

"Thank you, old friend. Mr. Jamison, as my Bosun, you have been in charge of my ship and my house since I have had one, I need you to continue to do so. Sometimes that may not be easy. We do not know what may come to our house in this venture. I know I can trust you to control whatever may happen here at home. Whether you wish to take part in things away from here will be up to you."

"I will certainly give it my best, Your Grace."

"Thank you. Davis, you worked hard and became one of my top men. We have had many adventures together. Are you ready for action again?"

"Aye, aye, Your Grace. Life has been a bit too quiet, I fancy an adventure," he replied with a salute and a grin.

"Well done, men. I will tell His Lordship, that we will take his mission in the morning, get a good night's sleep, what's left of it. We will have a planning meeting after His Lordship leaves in the morning. Jamison, it may be impossible to keep the household from knowing some of our business, so be sure everyone can be trusted."

"Most certainly, Your Grace."

Chapter Four: Planning

The next morning after breakfast in the Solarium, Vincent saw his friend off, then went to his office. He rang for a maid. When she arrived, he said, "Tell Mr. Jamison one o'clock in my office."

"Right away, Your Grace."

He proceeded to make his plans and start a list of his needs. His mind had been working things out since his first conversation with Simon. Now he had to be ready to explain things to his crew. When he finally looked at the clock, it was only eleven o'clock, he was better organized than he thought. He decided he had time for a walk before luncheon. He rang for a maid. When she arrived he said, "Tell Mr. Jamison that I would like luncheon in the garden in an hour."

She curtsied and replied, "Yes, Your Grace."

He left through his private door to the outside. It was a lovely day. His favorite walk was through the orchard. He stopped under the large apple tree. The fruit would be ready for harvest soon. He contemplated sitting on the bench under the tree but shook his head. Not today, he needed to walk, and he did want to think about Andrea. She had been the taming force in his life; however, he was sure she would approve of this venture.

He felt refreshed when he reached the garden and had a nice quiet lunch. Then he returned to his office and only had to wait a couple minutes before there was a knock on the door. "Enter."

Jamison, Riggs and Davis entered. He gestured for them to sit. He sat at his desk. "Any comments or changes of heart before I begin?"

Riggs and Davis shook their heads. Jamison spoke. "I have been thinking about the staff since our conversation last night. Would you like my report on them now or later?"

Vincent thought a few moments. "Now is a good time. We should know how secure we are before we start. Be detailed. Assume I know nothing about them."

Jamison looked a little flustered, "Well, Your Grace, I know you are very aware of everyone in our household, but you said you wanted details, so with your permission I will detail each one. Since we no longer entertain, we don't have a large staff; which is good at this point. Fewer people to worry about. We have never kept a large staff here as you and Her Grace liked your privacy. We always hired more staff as needed for dances, parties, and things. There are only seven who actually reside in house: my wife and I of course; Riggs; Davis; Molly the scullery; Betty the head housemaid; Nat a footman, and Mrs. Greer. The other two maids and footmen live in the village and come in during the day and as needed. Others who live on the property besides the tenants are the Baileys, cook and head groundskeeper; Edison, the gamekeeper and his men; your estate manager Jenkins; and the Stable Master, Liam and his two lads. Mr. Bailey has some lads come in to help him as needed."

Vincent nodded, "Yes, Mrs. Greer, Her Grace's lady's maid. I did not have the heart to let her go. She was with Andrea since her debut. I suppose I should give her a cottage and retire her."

Jamison nodded, but said, "True, Your Grace, but she has been very useful here in the house. She is quite a hand with a needle and keeps things repaired and makes things as needed. She has been content to continue to live here."

Vincent raised an eyebrow. "Yes, that could be very useful. If she is content with living in the house, let us continue with that. So how do you feel about them all?"

"I feel everyone is very loyal to you. You and Her Grace are very kind to your staff and the villagers. I don't think anyone would do anything that would endanger you in anyway. This village has always been closed mouth as to its business. I do not see that changing. Some of the lads would probably like to help out. The only one of any concern is the maid, Tessie, and only because she is such a ninny, she might say the wrong thing to the wrong person without thinking."

"Let us keep an eye on Tessie. I do not want to let people go if I do not have to. If you think it might become a problem, then I trust your judgement. How about the London House?"

"The only permanent staff who reside there is just the Handleys, as the house is usually closed unless you need it. You and Her Grace preferred to live here and seldom visited London. You only take who you need with you, so still no problems there. If you open the house, you can decide how you want to deal with staff."

"Very good. We will, unfortunately, need to use the London house, I am sure; but we will cross that bridge when necessary. The Handleys are officially retired and just look after the place, I do not think we need to tell them anything at this point."

Jamison remarked, "I might make a suggestion, Your Grace. We might alert the gamekeepers to keep an eye out for strangers. They are usually pretty alert, but an extra precaution might not go awry. They do not need to know why at this point. Just that you want to insure your privacy."

"Good point. I shall let you handle that."

"Of course, Your Grace. I shall attend to it as soon as we are finished."

"Very good. Well, gentlemen, I have decided the first major thing we need is a proper ship. I have the yacht, but we need something bigger, that can sail anywhere we want to go and carry passengers if need be. Our first assignment is a piracy problem in Guernsey. It is and then it is not part of England. Smuggling has become a good income for them, but a pirate has become a problem for them and the Crown. So we get to sort it out. The ... shall we call him 'our benefactor' ... I am sure would like the whole smuggling business stopped, but those people survive on it. I have been told to solve things as I see fit. That may not always make our benefactor happy, because I will not do anything I do not consider true justice and we know the law is not always just. If our benefactors do not like the way we handle things, they can just find someone else. That being said, Riggs, you and I will find us a ship. Jamison and Davis, I need you to start compiling a list of people to help us, we need some young, strong lads and we will need some who are seaworthy. Davis, when you are done with that, take a good lad or two and do some reconnaissance in Guernsey. Jamison, if you need more funds in your household stash, let me know."

Chapter Five: Ready

Three weeks later Vincent sailed into the harbor near the estate. While the new crew was unloading their cargo from the new Dutch schooner, Vincent and Riggs walked to the house. Jamison welcomed them at the door, "Good to have you back, Your Grace. Davis sent a messenger. He is helping out in the stables while we waited for you."

He was having a hard time not staring at His Grace. His Grace had always been a very conservative man, dressing soberly and appropriately for his station. The man who now entered the house was almost unknown to him. He was still dressed in black as befitted his mourning period, but now quite the dandy. His coat and breeches were black velvet, his waistcoat was black satin, his shirt was black silk with black lace flowing out from the very large satin cuffs. His black silk cravat was also quite lacy and flowed down the front of his shirt. His tricorn was quite ornate with black feathers.

Vincent was well aware that he had startled his butler, but ignored the fact for the moment. "Bring him to my office. I wish to see you as well." He and Riggs went to the office, leaving the door open.

Ten minutes later, Jamison and a young man appeared at the door. Vincent waved them in. "Come in and close the door."

Once inside, Jamison said, "This is Ian. We recruited him from the village. He went to Guernsey with Davis."

Vincent looked at the lad, "Davis sent you with a message?"

Ian nodded, "Aye, Your Grace. He said to tell you 'e and Carter are settled in. 'Ave jobs in a couple pubs, Le Marais and the Queen Charlotte Inn. The Queen Charlotte seems to be a haunt for sea captains, and they do get into their cups and love to boast of their deeds," he said smiling.

"Very well, we will sail to Guernsey. We always have to assume someone may have heard of us. So we must be aware of that. We have all played parts before. As you see I have decided to become quite the fop. I have noticed that type of person seldom gets taken seriously and I do not want people to think I am serious about anything anymore. No one will suspect us doing any harm. We will sail to Guernsey. We will be in search of contraband for our own pleasure. I should attract attention throwing money around."

The men laughed. "What do you want of us?" asked Riggs.

"Jamison, I need you to check out the crew we picked up to sail the ship. We found some old friends from our past in Hampshire and I am sure they will do. We made it here on our own; but we need a few more. They need to be able to defend themselves if necessary. We should have ten to eleven to sail her comfortably, see if any of the village lads are interested. As soon as I decided I wanted a ship, I sent word to our benefactor that we need Certificates of Exemption. I don't need any of our sailors taken from us and pressed into service with the Navy. Those should arrive soon, and we will not leave without them."

"Jamison, I think this time I would like you to accompany us, as you can use purchasing provisions for my household as a reason to see what is going on. Along with a solid bunch of sailors, Davis and his lads, Riggs and I, we shall be able to accomplish the task."

Jamison nodded, "As you wish, Your Grace."

"Riggs, I need you and Mrs. Greer to revamp my wardrobe. I am in mourning, so it should be all black, but I need to be quite the dandy. If we can do without a tailor for now, I would prefer it. After this problem is settled, we will go to London to establish my new self and go shopping." He looked at his men and winked. "Are we ready for this new adventure,"

They all smiled. Jamison, Davis and Riggs said, "Aye, Aye, Captain."

Ian looked confused, but nodded and replied, "Yes Your Grace."

Chapter Six: Alderney

One week later, they were sailing into Alderney. Vincent had decided that they would use the Queen Charlotte Inn as a headquarters during their visit as Davis had said it was the best place for them to be. After they landed, he sent Riggs to acquire a private dining room for their use while in port. His ship was well outfitted for his purposes and he had no intention of inconveniencing himself by spending the nights in an inn. It didn't fit his new image. He would take Riggs with him for a valet and secretary as he went about as was appropriate of his rank, a couple of sturdy lads as guards and leave the rest of the crew on board the ship to be ready as needed. They would remain around the dock and keep their ears open for any tidbits that might be useful. Jamison and Ilya would take a few lads with them as they set out on excursions looking for special items for His Grace's table.

Ilya had been a stroke of good luck. He had been an assistant in one of His Grace's favorite London restaurants, but had been in the wrong place at the wrong time and was pressed into His Majesty's Navy. Jamison had heard about the situation when he was looking for sailors. Vincent managed with the aid of their benefactor to rescue him.

Later their first day in port, Vincent received a message from Matthew Andros, a gentleman of some import on the island.

'Your Grace,

What a delight to have you visit our little island. I am sure you find the inn beneath your standards, and my wife Anne and I would be honored for you to take your residence with us while you are on the island.

Your servant,

Matthew Andros'

Vincent had done his research and knew that Andros had purchased some French Corsairs with his wife's money and was well entrenched with the Privateers. Not wanting to offend the gentleman, but also not wanting to so limit his actions, he returned what he hoped was a conciliatory note.

'Mr. Andros,

I do so appreciate your very gracious invitation. However, I am here with a rather large contingency. We have been told that this is a wonderful place to find those special things that make life so bearable, so I plan to do a lot of shopping. I am afraid I will distress your household with my activities. Perhaps, you and your lovely wife might find time to dine with me tomorrow evening at nine o'clock aboard my ship *The Fair Wind?*

Vincent Pomeroy, Duke of Edgingham'

Andros was a bit distressed by the response to his invitation. However, he would not dare to turn down His Grace's invitation to dine. The ship was docked, rather than anchored out in the bay, so it would be an easy thing for his wife to board. He quickly returned his acceptance.

Vincent and his crew were already busy looking into the best places to find smuggled goods. Vincent was relying on Rigg's good judgement when it came to materials, linens, wool, lace, cotton, silks and satins as they were available in different qualities. Riggs could always pick the best. Jamison was well trained to pick the best wines, brandies and spirits. Everyone was looking for frivolous things that one should look for when buying from smugglers.

Well before the streets darkened with the coming of night, they made their way back to the ship. Once on board, they doubled security for the night and made themselves comfortable. Ilya had fixed them a wonderful late dinner. Vincent didn't want to stand on ceremony and dinner was a good time to share information, so Jamison, Ilya, Riggs and Davis joined him at table. Davis had been hired away from the inn during the day by Riggs and was glad to be working for the Duke rather than slaving away at the inn.

Once everyone had been served, Vincent asked, "So what has everyone learned of use today?"

Jamison reported, "No mention of the pirate that is disrupting the smuggling, but it does not take much to learn that smuggling is a great source of income here in the Channel Islands."

Vincent laughed, "Yes, the Captains at the inn are quite bold with their bragging and throwing their money around. They were wary of me at first, but then word got around that I'm buying, and their tongues loosened."

Davis then laughed, "I did my best to spread the rumor that I heard you were quite rich and liked to throw your money around. These people are wary but want to earn a quick quid. Those off shore reefs help protect the islands and make this a good smuggling haven."

His Grace nodded. "Yes, Les Ecrehous and Les Minquiers are quite wicked."

Davis added, "The people feel that what comes here is nobody's business but theirs. If the taxmen question them, Captains often say twas a 'contrary wind' that kept them from having their ship examined for cargo." They all laughed. "People with any money at all chipped in and bought ships for a piece of the prize. Did not take long before this whole area was doing quite well on smuggled goods and captured cargo ships."

Riggs replied, "I've heard St. Brelade's Bay is the best location for them to unload and there are tricky caves on Sark to hide contraband."

Vincent considered all that. "I do not think it will be necessary for us to wander about and maybe get in trouble. I think it best we plant ourselves at the Queen Charlotte and let them come to us. We have established ourselves as buyers and we will learn what we want to know. I have invited Andros and his wife to dine tomorrow evening. I want to impress them that I am fop with funds galore. So let us do it up to the extreme. It is well known that he uses his wife's money to promote his Privateers and has done very nicely with it."

Ilya beamed. "I shall do you proud, mon Capitan."

Vincent lifted his glass to him and smiled. "I have no doubt of that."

The next day, they all went about their business as befitted their ruse of looking for special deals. Ilya was out early to get supplies for the special dinner he had planned. Everyone would be on their own for the rest of the day, appearing to be at leisure. Vincent ventured out to a few shops, but mostly held court at the inn. People learned of his reason for being there and as he expected, found their way to him.

He returned to the ship before dark to prepare for his guests. Riggs helped him dress in his fanciest evening attire. He took a last look in his mirror and shook his head. He was wearing black velvet knee britches with a long black velvet coat, black satin waistcoat, black silk shirt with black lace hanging from his sleeves to almost his finger-tips. His jabot was also frothy with lace. It quite filled the front of his shirt. He wore long black stockings and shoes with gold buckles. "My gracious, that is so far overdone, how am I supposed to eat?"

Riggs chuckled. "May I suggest your very large diamond stick pin on your jabot. It will scream money and help hold your lace from getting in your way. You said you wished to look the fop, I have done my best."

Vincent nodded. "You have done well, my friend. You have done very well."

When Matthew and Anne Andros arrived promptly at nine, they were greeted by Jamison in his proper butler attire. They were extremely impressed by how well the ship was outfitted. It was definitely a luxury traveling ship, not the usual fare. They were shown into His Grace's presence in his sitting room, which though small, was nicely outfitted as if it were in his home, not aboard a ship.

"Mr. and Mrs. Andros, Your Grace," announced Jamison. They both made their proper obeisance.

"Welcome," Vincent said as he kissed Mrs. Andros' hand. "Please be seated. I am so delighted to be visiting your little island. I have heard such wonderful things about it. I do so love shopping and have heard that it is a great adventure here."

"Most assuredly, Your Grace," replied Mr. Andros. "Trade ships come in here daily bringing such a wonderful variety of goods. I am sure we can find things to please you."

At that moment, Jamison announced dinner and Vincent escorted Mrs. Andros, followed by her husband into his small but well equipped dining room. A large silver candelabra surrounded by local flowers graced the center of the table. The table was set with china, silver and crystal. It was not at all what they expected to find on a traveling ship. Mrs. Andros was quite taken back, "What a lovely setting," she exclaimed. "I find your quarters are quite comfortable, unlike the ones on other ships where I have been. How do you do it?"

"I do so love my creature comforts. If one is going to travel, one should be quite at ease, do you not agree?" answered Vincent as she was seated on his right by Davis. He indicated for Mr. Andros to sit to his left. "I prefer to bring the comforts of home with me. It does take a bit more trouble, but that is why one has servants, is it not?"

Conversation during dinner consisted of information about their beautiful island, gossip from

England, and clothes. He wanted to be sure the lady was amused. Jamison and Davis served them, with some assistance from one of the deck hands who was wearing His Grace's proper livery. Ilya had outdone himself with separate courses of turtle soup, oyster patties, lobster in a lovely wine sauce, and fried artichokes. The chef himself served his main course of Roast Duck a la Orange. Vincent took a bite, then said, "I say, Ilya, this is fabulous. You have outdone yourself." Ilya beamed.

Mrs. Andros also stated, "My goodness, how can you make such a delight with only a ship's galley? My cook certainly cannot compare and we have a very large kitchen." Mr. Andros was too busy stuffing himself and just nodded.

"Ilya can work culinary miracles anywhere," replied Vincent. Jamison finished serving the delectable lemon pudding with whipped cream and the final savory of beef cheeks in a spicy tomato sauce. His Grace was pleased to see that his guests seemed quite impressed with the special repast, noticing Mrs. Andros really seemed to enjoy her dinner rather than pick at her food like most ladies. He was sure it was because it was such fine cuisine, rather than a healthy appetite. She was loathe to miss out just to be a dainty, proper lady. He was also quite sure she would make good use of the bragging rights for being invited to dine at the table of a Duke.

Once they were finished, he said, "Since it is just the three of us, I suggest we repair to the sitting room for coffee and port." They moved back into the sitting room, where Jamison served the gentlemen port and coffee for Mrs. Andros. "I hope I won't bore you, my dear, but I am most curious about the wonderful goods that are so available here."

Mr. Andros smiled slyly, "I am sure Your Grace knows our island income is from imports, mainly from Privateers. We are sanctioned by the Crown and pay our taxes."

Vincent smiled. "I am sure you do. I do not trouble myself with the government. That which they are unaware of cannot give us any grief. Since my wife died, I just can't bear London. I have preferred to be a recluse at my country estate, but recently a friend brought me out of my ennui. He said, I should find something to divert me from my woe. So I pulled myself together and came up with a brilliant idea. I loved being at sea when I was younger, so I decided to buy myself a ship and travel to where ever I wish. However, I have heard rumors of a true pirate in these waters. That does strike terror into one's heart. What do you know of this? Am I in any danger? I have no wish for any trouble."

"Do not concern yourself, Your Grace. I have my ships on alert. I am sure we will catch this interloper. Rumor has it that he is of French origin and he does seem to attack from that direction. However, he does seem to pick on those who are not in a position to complain, if you understand me, Your Grace."

"Hmm. I am sure I do. I still find the situation rather distressful. I do feel safe here on the island, so I will probably stay awhile, if that will not be of concern to anyone. I fear a personal ship of one such as I might be too juicy a plum for some marauder. It chills me to the very bone." He shuddered. "But, I fear we are distressing Mrs. Andros with such conversation. Let us move on to more interesting things. Where does one find the best shopping? I am desirous of some of the finery so well done in France, but do not desire to have to go there. And I have heard this is the place for finding the best Brandy and delightful wines."

The conversation turned to places and people who might provide such things to His Grace's pleasure. Finally the ships' bells signaled it was midnight and His Grace mocked a stiffled yawn. "I do express my regrets, but I am afraid after my long lethargy, I tire rather easily. I do hope you do not mind if I require an early evening." He rose.

"Not at all, Your Grace," replied Mr. Andros quickly coming to his feet and holding out his hand to assist his wife. "We are honored by your invitation and hope you will accept ours to a small party we are having on Saturday. It will be just a small gathering for dinner and dancing. We do hope you will be able to join us."

"Oh, that sounds quite lovely. I certainly accept your kind invitation."

"And I will check with my contacts and find you some good places for you to fulfill your shopping list. I will call upon you at the Queen Charlotte, when I have news."

"That is very kind of you. Please join me for lunch at the inn any time. I am afraid Chef Ilya does not do lunch when we are ashore. It was the final plum to steal him away. Just money was not enough. He wanted time to himself as well." With that he escorted his guests to the gangplank and saw them safely off in their carriage. After that, they secured for the night.

Late the next afternoon, Mr. Andros appeared at the inn. He approached the sailor stationed at the open door to the private sitting room the Duke had secured. "I have some news for His Grace."

The sailor nodded, entered the room and spoke to Riggs who was sitting at a table near His Grace taking some notes. Riggs looked up at His Grace who appeared to be ignoring the doorway. "Mr. Andros desires to speak with you, Your Grace." Vincent merely nodded and looked toward the doorway.

"Mr. Andros," he gushed as he waved the man in. "I did not expect to see you so soon."

Mr. Andros bowed appropriately and entered the room. The sailor returned to his station at the door. Mr. Andros looked around as he was not sure about speaking freely. The patrons of the inn were just at tables in the other room and could hear what was happening in here if they wished to pay attention, and he was sure at least some of them would. "I … ah … promised to find you some items you were looking for. I believe you will be pleased. I had them delivered to my warehouse to save you a dangerous trip. It is just a short walk."

Vincent was disappointed, he wanted to see where these things were kept, but he understood the security. He turned to Riggs, "Please get Jamison and some men and join us." Riggs hurried from the room and returned half an hour later with Jamison and four large sailors who were well armed with pistols and swords. "We are ready," said Vincent when all were assembled.

Mr. Andros hesitated. He remarked, "You do not need guards, Your Grace, it is just a short walk to my warehouse. Quite a public place."

Riggs replied, "His Grace does not wander around the docks unprotected. Everyone knows that he carries gold."

Mr. Andros looked abashed and nodded, "Of course."

They exited the inn and made the short walk and found many splendors: silks, satins, wool, cottons, lace, brandy and wines from France, tobacco, spices. The men who brought them had priced them well and knew it and weren't into bargaining, though Jamison tried. "Don't bother yourself, Jamison. You and Riggs get what we want. I can afford it. Their prices are more than fair. Be sure to get some imported cottons since they are banned in England."

Mr. Andros pulled him aside to a small area with a few small chests. "Perhaps Your Grace would be interested in some fine jewelry, for yourself or a lady friend. We had the pleasure of relieving a Spanish cargo ship of some special treasures bound for Madrid. Spanish ships are fair game, nothing nefarious there."

Vincent understood perfectly. The Spanish and the English had been at odds for centuries and still were. Spanish ships were fair game for just about everyone. The only fly in the ointment was that the British authorities preferred prize ships, those ships captured and taken by the privateers, be brought into an official port and 'condemned'. This would put it under their jurisdiction so they could charge tax on the goods and take the ship for a small part of its value. Privateers made more money on their own. He had heard the men in the inn talk about being prevented from taking ships to these ports by what Davis had called 'a contrary wind'. He picked a few pieces for gifts for his sister and for himself. In his new role as a Dandy, he could use some fancy pieces.

After hanging about in Alderney for a week and not really gaining any knowledge toward their mission, they left port and tried a few other islands, still to no avail.

Chapter Seven: Pirates

Once they docked in St. Peter Port and everything was settled in for the night, they sat at dinner, discussing the problem. Vincent told his staff, "We' have been in this area over a fortnight and no sign of trouble. Before we arrived, our pirate was marauding at least every other night, if not every night. I thought sure we would have heard news of him."

Davis replied, "I was sure when we left Alderney and were sailing about the islands, he would have attacked us. Surely he heard we were worth the trouble."

Riggs replied, "Maybe he only likes to attack smugglers, maybe he has it in for them. Maybe he is jealous."

Jamison answered, "I think he is afraid of us. Something about us worries him. Does he know who we are? Who are his spies? What about us makes him stay his hand?"

"Mr. Andros said he seems to strike those who can not complain. We do not fit that description. Let us look at a map after dinner and see if we can sort out what we know about where he strikes. Maybe just wandering around is not good enough."

After dinner, they all quickly cleared the table and pulled out the map of the Channel area. Vincent threw a handful of coins on the table. "Mark the areas where we know he has attacked." The men quickly put coins on those areas where they had heard of the attacks. Once they were done, it was very obvious. He didn't strike within the islands, only on the outskirts, where ships were coming in from France or headed out for England.

"Gentlemen, I think we change course for France, at a leisurely pace, of course. I believe I find myself in need of some French fashion," said Vincent in his foppish style. "Set sail for Le Havre, then we will at least appear to be going to Paris."

Everyone laughed. "Aye, aye, sir," they all responded.

Two days later, after they had taken on supplies, they set sail for France. They gave the Cap de la Hague a wide berth in hope of attracting their prey, but as nothing happened, Vincent decided to anchor in the Baio de la Seine for the evening. They enjoyed a quiet dinner and a lovely evening sitting on deck making plans for the coming raid. Before retiring, Jamison and Vincent made sure the deck was well guarded and lookouts posted.

The light tap on his cabin door awakened Vincent immediately. He did not speak, just got up and opened the door. One of the sentries was standing there. He did not speak either, just nodded his head in the direction of the main deck. Vincent merely grabbed a jacket as he had gone to bed dressed in breeches and a loose shirt, ready for action. They hurried on deck, staying in the shadows. The moon was playing hide and seek in the cloudy sky. The sentry pointed toward the northwest toward Cherbourg. Vincent could see a few deck lights of a ship. As they watched, the ship drew closer and the lights went out.

They stayed out of their own lanterns and he could feel his men quietly taking their places as pre-arranged. This pirate was about to meet his doom. From his men's information, they did not use their cannons, just quietly boarded ships or rammed into small crafts. Cannon fire would attract too much attention from the shore. Plus from the information accumulated, Vincent discerned that they probably were unaccustomed to much resistance. Smugglers did not want to attract attention, so defended themselves with knives when needed, and were not prepared for boarding by pirates. Vincent hoped this would work to their advantage. The men had all been instructed to allow the pirates to board, and then to take them down.

It seemed forever, till they felt the other ship bump into theirs. They were stationed so grappling hooks would not harm any of them. As the pirates boarded *The Fair Wind*, they found themselves quickly engaged in defending themselves. Vincent's men soon had the upper hand and boarded the pirate ship and took it over. Vincent had been correct, they were not used to much resistance.

Although Vincent had been very involved in the fray, as soon as the rogue Captain was brought before him, he immediately reverted to his persona. "I say, that was jolly unfriendly of you. Look what you have done to my ship. Just look at the damage to the railing from those ugly hooks. I think you definitely owe me an explanation."

The Captain looked Vincent up and down, like he was some kind of freak. "Just who are you?" he demanded.

"The question is who are you? I know who I am. If it had not been for my marvelous crew, you would have taken my lovely ship. Just who do you think you are?"

"I don't have to answer to the likes of you. You are a nobody. I rule these seas and take what I want."

Vincent raised an eyebrow. "Does not look to me like you rule anything. You are my captive. We will just take you to back to the Governor of Guernsey and let him deal with you. I do not think you will be very popular there." He turned to Jamison. "Take him away," waving his hand. "Tie them all up. Put some men on his ship and we will take it with us to Guernsey. I am sure there is a nice reward for both ship and those … those ruffians.

No, wait. He owes me restitution. Take Riggs and make a full inventory of our losses, including ruined clothes," he said looking down at himself and gesturing to his own clothes. One of his opponents had managed to skewer his jacket, however, he was unharmed.

Jamison grinned, "Aye, aye, Your Grace."

The pirate Captain's eyes widened. "Your Grace?"

"Yes," replied Jamison, "You have the honor of being captured by His Grace, Vincent Pomeroy, Duke of Edgingham. Take this pile of garbage away."

Three days later, they were sailing away from the Channel Islands. Vincent was ready for some quiet time at home. He called Riggs, Jamison and Davis to his cabin. "Davis, we shall stop at Portsmouth and send you to London with my report. I have told our benefactor that he can trust all of you implicitly. If he has another adventure for us, you can bring word to me at home. I am not ready to spend time in London yet."

Chapter Eight: Jacob

A month later found them in Edinburgh. Rumor had it that Charles Stuart was looking to cause problems for the Crown. Vincent was not sure how he felt about this issue, but he did not mind a little spying. Shopping was always a good excuse to travel and shop clerks loved to gossip. On the way to Edinburgh, he remembered an old Navy colleague who was Scottish, and he believed he was from that area. After they were settled at the Inn, he asked, "Riggs, I believe I know someone from this area. See if you can fine Lord Jacob McClaren. You might remember him as well, he traveled with us aboard ship several times."

Riggs nodded, "Yes, I remember him, quiet young man, did not really mix with the crew. Would come aboard, kept himself to himself, then quietly leave at some port. I will see what I can learn."

He returned later that afternoon. "Your Grace, I have news of your friend."

"Good, well do not keep me in suspense, is he near here?"

"Actually, Your Grace, he is in town. He has been in town for some weeks. His wife died and he has been here in Edinburgh since. Keeps himself to himself, nothing new about that. The family's estate is not far from here. The old Duke runs the Clan like a tight ship. Both parents are still living, as well as one older brother. Your friend has a son who lives on the family property and a daughter in Glasgow."

"Very good, Riggs. Excellent job as always. I will send him a message at once."

"I will deliver it myself, Your Grace."

"Wonderful, wait for a response, please."

'Lord McClaren,

I find myself in your beautiful Scotland. I would be very pleased to spend some time in your

company if that would not be intruding on your mourning.

Vincent Pomeroy, Duke of Edginham'

Riggs returned with a reply quite promptly.

'Your Grace,

I would be delighted to see you again, however since the loss of my wife, I prefer not to go out. Please come dine with me this evening. We have much to discuss. I usually dine early, would six o'clock be convenient?

McClaren'

Vincent smiled when he received the reply. *Yes, I think we have much to discuss.* He responded immediately. "Riggs, send this with a messenger. It does not need your personal attention since I do not require a reply."

'McClaren,

Six o'clock is most convenient. I look forward to our visit.

Pomeroy'

Vincent arrived promptly at six. He was greeted at the door by a butler who showed him to the library. McClaren rose as Vincent entered the room. "It is good to see you again, Your Grace."

"Please, call me Vincent. First, I want to express my condolences on the loss of your wife. I, too, have lost mine. It is a very life changing event."

"I would be honored to do so, and you must call me Jacob. Thank you for your condolence. I'm still at a loss. I suppose it takes time to adjust to it."

"It does indeed. It has been a long time since you would catch a ride on my ship when you were on missions. It is good to see you again."

Jacob had to admit that he was a little shocked at the appearance of his former colleague. He remembered Pomeroy as the very efficient Captain, quite the manly man, but now he appeared to have become over dressed, very much the dandy … well there was no other word for it, very foppish. Had the loss of his wife changed him that much?

It was only a few minutes until the butler announced dinner. They spent the meal reminiscing about old times and catching up on family and their new situations in life.

"Margaret's illness was long and rough, but we battled it together," Jacob told him. "I resigned my commission when it was evident that her illness was serious. After she died, I just couldn't bear to stay in that house. My parents are very upset with me. Father wanted me to stay on the estate and help with things. Since my oldest brother was killed in the Fifteen, I am his spare. I do not care. I just can not do it. He has Dougal, my older brother. My son, Jake, will gladly help out. Mother just likes having her family quite near. Now I just have to find something to do with myself. I cannot just sit and do nothing."

Vincent replied, "I so understand. When Andrea was killed by that highwayman, I thought my world had ended. We were a love match. A friend came to my rescue and pulled me from my ennui, suggested I find other pursuits. I've always loved sailing, so I bought a ship, and I've learned I love shopping. So away I go. I am sure something will come to you to occupy you as well."

Vincent waited until after dinner, when they were sitting in the privacy and comfort of the library to broach the subject of his new venture. Up to that point he had kept his ruse of the Dandy. After Jacob poured them each a brandy, Vincent said, "I do have something of import I wish to discuss with you. After Andrea died, I was offered the opportunity to do something that I would like to offer to you, but I must have your promise of total silence on the subject."

Jacob looked askance at him. What could His Grace possibly be doing of interest to him? "I, of course, would never betray a confidence."

Vincent laughed and dropped his ruse. "Do not let the clothes and this ruse fool you. I am deadly serious. I have been asked to do some secret missions for the Home Office. I have total autonomy over whom I do them with and how they are done. I would value your assistance with this project. I think we can make some differences in our world and we would deal very well together." He smiled. "As to this," he said, waving his hand over himself, "I find it very useful for looking quite innocent. No one expects a Dandy to be dangerous." He laughed at the look on Jacob's face. "I would not expect you to do the same."

"While I enjoyed the military at one time, I do not know that I would enjoy it again. I did a lot of things I am not proud of. I do not wish to do that kind of thing again."

"Good, then you will like this. As I said, I have complete autonomy. I can take or refuse to take any mission. These are things that our country does not officially want to meddle in. They want someone to handle them, but they can not be involved. They asked me. I told them I would, but only if I do things as I see fit. My attitude is that if they do not like it, then they should not ask me to take care of it. I just finished the first one. They must not be too distressed with me as they sent me here." He laughed.

"What can you tell me of your recent adventure?"

Vincent laughed again. "Just sorted out a problem with a pirate. It was actually kind of fun. It has been awhile since I have had to do sword play. I think I should take up fencing lessons again, I have gotten a little rusty. I could be quite the swashbuckler, do you not think?" He smiled, then looked serious. "I am quite sure they would have liked me to find a way to stop the smuggling, but that is impossible. Those people depend on it for their survival. It is an important part of their lives. The government just wants their share, but that is their problem, not mine. Right now we are just doing a little spying. Getting the lay of the land here in Scotland."

"I would not want to be involved in anything against my conscience," replied Jacob.

"No need for you to be. As I said, we can pick and choose our involvement."

Jacob nodded. "I find that very interesting, but I would like some time to think on it."

"I would expect no less of you."

"How long are you staying in Edinburgh? You are in no hurry to return home, are you?"

Vincent shook his head, "However long I choose. My time is my own."

"Good, you are quite welcome to stay here. I have plenty of room."

"That would be very kind of you. I do not relish staying at an inn, but it was preferable to the ship for our purposes. I would most welcome your hospitality."

Jacob laughed. "Yes, a good inn is acceptable for a night or two and staying aboard a ship would definitely not be my preference."

Vincent gave him a sly smile. "Wait till you see my ship. I have made it most comfortable, but this time staying aboard did not put us in the thick of things. With your permission, I will head back to my lodgings and we shall come join you tomorrow. I am only traveling with my valet this trip."

"I rise early, so please come, whenever you like. Actually, if you rise early, why not join me for a ride. I have not been out and about much since I arrived in town, but I do go out early for a ride for some exercise. I brought some good horses with me."

"Thank you. I would enjoy that. I will see you, say seven?"

"Perfect."

The next morning after their ride, they enjoyed a hearty breakfast. Afterwards when comfortable seated in the library, Jacob said, "I would like to discuss your proposal."

"You have my undivided attention."

"A part of me is very interested, I do not look forward to life here without Margaret. I did always enjoy the cloak and dagger. Some of this would not be much different than my military career, secret missions, clandestine meetings, silent spying. The main problem with war is innocent people get hurt, killed. I do not want to be a part of that again. Defending my property and family is one thing, seeking out evil doers and disposing of them is most acceptable, but I do not like it if innocents get hurt.

If we go into this without that consideration, I am not interested."

Vincent nodded his head. "I totally understand. I do not plan on taking any missions of that nature. That is why I was most insistent that I control the outcome. There are always situations we cannot control. People will do the damnedest things at the most inopportune moments, but our goal is to control that as much as possible."

"On that we can most certainly agree. Count me in."

Vincent rose to his feet and stretched out his hand to Jacob. The two men shook hands. He smiled. "I am most pleased to have you with us." Vincent resumed his seat. "We could use some more trustworthy men. I have three who have been with me a long time. You may recognize them, although you didn't mingle with the crew much. Can you recommend a few?"

Jacob was thoughtful for a few minutes. "I am sure Angus will join me. We have been friends since childhood. He loved the military life. He stayed in longer than I. He will relish some adventure. He is actually due here tomorrow. We can talk to him then." He chuckled. "And I just might I know of a couple more. There are two young men in the clan who might be interested, William and Benjamin. Their fathers quite despair of them. They are good lads, but neither like dealing with their farms and want more adventure. They tend to find themselves in trouble occasionally out of boredom. This is just the thing for them."

Chapter Nine: A New Mission

The next morning as they arrived back at the house after their ride, a stable lad informed them a messenger had arrived for the Duke and was in the kitchen. They left their horses with the lad and started back to the house. Jacob asked, "Would you have any objection to going in through the kitchen. It is closer than walking all the way around to the front. I am sure you are anxious for your news."

"If it will not shock your staff, that would be fine with me."

"I do it all the time. I am much less formal when I am here on my own. I used to always enter through the kitchen after my morning ride and steal goodies from Mrs. Broddock. She'll be delighted that I am up to my old tricks," Jacob answered laughing.

Entering the kitchen, they found Davis having breakfast. He immediately rose to his feet. Vincent raised an eyebrow and commented, "Davis, did not expect to see you so quickly."

"Sorry Your Grace, but I have a message from London."

"Very well." He looked at Jacob. "May we adjourn to your office?"

Jacob nodded. "Of course."

All three men immediately went to the office. Jacob went to his desk and indicated for Vincent to take a comfortable chair. Jacob looked at Davis and said, "Davis, please sit down. You look tired."

Davis looked from His Grace to Lord McClaren and back to His Grace. He was obviously unsure of what to do. Vincent smiled. "It is all right, Davis, you may sit down. You may speak freely in front of Lord McClaren. He is now one of us."

Davis nodded. He handed His Grace a letter. "He came to see us ... at the house, Your Grace. He asked that we deal with this as soon as we possibly could. He did say that he understood it would take some time to prepare for this one and extra travel time, whatever that means."

Vincent quickly read the letter and handed it to Jacob. "So, problems in Jamaica? Yes, that will take some extra preparation. It is a long voyage. They just want us to see what the situation really is. They want an outsider's opinion. Our government officials there have been reporting that it has things under control, but the British landowners say that the locals ... What did he call them?"

Jacob was reading while he was listening to Vincent. "He calls them Maroons."

"Well the landowners are saying they are still a problem. They have a new interim governor. Our benefactor wants assurance that the situation is under control. If tis not, well, we do not have to anything, just hurry back and let him know." Vincent sat thinking for a few minutes. He looked at Jacob. "Well, are you in for this one or do you want to wait? I have a good excuse to go to Jamaica. My son, Alistair is there with friends."

Jacob finished reading the letter. "It has been a long time since I was in Jamaica. Just a short stop on the way to the colonies. I think I would like to go again."

"Sugarcane is a valuable crop. We can use investing in it as your reason for being there."

"Good idea," replied Jacob.

Vincent nodded. "I will get started supplying the ship for the voyage. Are you going to ask Angus to join us? What about your young men?"

"Angus, most definitely. I am sure he will relish the adventure. I will wait to ask Will and Ben as it may take more time than we have to sort them out."

Vincent was nodding. "I should like to be away as soon as we can be ready. I will need a short stop at home to change out some things."

"Sounds good," replied Jacob. "I suggest Davis go finish his breakfast while you and I have ours, then I think we all have a lot to do."

"Davis, I will notify Riggs of our plans. So have your breakfast and be prepared to leave. We will spend the day at the ship."

During breakfast Jacob and Vincent discussed things they would need for their journey. Vincent said, "I shall make sure we are well provisioned. We should be able to find most everything we need here in Edinburgh. The ship is well armed with any weapons we might need. Pirates are still a threat heading into the Caribbean. All you and Angus need to bring is your personal things and anything you might need or want on the journey. You should come visit the ship today so you can see for yourself how comfortable we shall be."

"That is probably a good idea. We shall do so after Angus arrives."

"Do not expect to be served luncheon. Ilya does not fix a midday meal when we are in port. We will forgive him that since he is fabulous the rest of the time," replied Vincent.

About one o'clock, Vincent was told that a carriage had arrived at the dock in front of the ship. He arrived at the top of the gangplank as Jacob and another man were approaching the dock side. The man was carrying a large basket.

"I thought we would bring you lunch," called Jacob.

Vincent laughed. "For that, you are most welcome. Come aboard."

Arriving on board, Jacob said, "Your Grace, this is my friend and clansman, Angus McClaren. Angus this is His Grace the Duke of Edgingham."

As Angus' hands were full, Vincent merely nodded. "Good to meet you. Please call me Vincent."

Angus nodded. "I am just Angus."

"We greatly appreciate the invitation to join you on your voyage. The prospect of doing trade in Jamaica is always interesting," said Jacob, not knowing who might hear them.

"Good, I hope it will be prosperous for all of us," replied Vincent

Vincent sent the sailors off to a tavern to get something to eat. The three of them found something to sit on, boxes and kegs were readily available as the ship was being loaded, and a large crate for a table and enjoyed their lunch. Mrs. Braddock had sent beef sandwiches, little chicken pies, and scones with clotted cream.

After stuffing themselves with the delicious lunch, Vincent showed them around the ship. Angus and Jacob left after a couple hours and Vincent joined them at home later for dinner and the evening.

The next day, Jacob and Angus arrived at the ship ready to go. They brought a cart with their gear and a few supplies that Jacob figured an Englishman would not know a Scotsman had need of. They had brought haggis, neeps, salmon, black pudding, grouse, venison, and Cook had made them some fresh scones, tablets and shortbread.

They left with the tide the next day, sailing down the coast to the harbor near Vincent's estate. It did not take them long to unload supplies he had bought for home and anything else they did not need for their journey, and bring aboard things they required from home for the longer journey. They were off with the next tide. Vincent also made sure they had fresh fruits and vegetables, especially limes and lemons as the men would need to drink a tablespoon of the juice a day to prevent scurvy. He decided that he would leave Jamison in England to look after things, but he would take Davis and Riggs with him. Jamison was quite pleased with this decision.

A week later, found them in the Canary Islands. Vincent and Jacob decided not to spend too much time there, but only made sure they resupplied their ship. They laid in supplies of bananas, tomatoes, peppers, green beans, potatoes, goat's milk, meat, eggs, chickens, and of course more lemons and limes. After a couple days there, they sailed toward Cape Verde until they caught the trade winds and made for the Caribbean. Fortune smiled on them and they had good weather and winds for most of their journey, only getting caught in a couple of short calms. They arrived in Antigua three weeks after their stop in the Canaries.

Chapter Ten: Jamaica

The whole ship was ready for some time on shore when they arrived in Antigua. The rest of their journey would be short hops, so they spent a few days in port getting their land legs and catching up on any news of the area. They also resupplied their ship, especially fresh fruits and vegetables, being sure to get some of the delicious sweet potatoes of the area. These were different from the ones they were accustomed to eating as they were white with a firmer flesh, but still quite delicious. The men had not seen some of the unusual fruits of the area, the soursop, rambutan, padoo, kamranga, and cowa to name a few. They looked very strange but were quite tasty. There were avocadoes, pears, mangos, a wide variety of apples and pears, bananas, plus cashews and almonds.

As to news of Jamaica, it was mostly of the maroon revolts and problems. The British were trying to control the problems, but it did not sound like they were succeeding. Vincent and Jacob did some inquiries into trade with sugarcane plantations, just to look legitimate. They left Antiqua three days later, making a leisurely journey across the islands, stopping in San Juan, Puerto Rico, and Port au Prince, Haiti, also making inquiries about the sugar trade, arriving five days later in Kingston, Jamaica.

Upon landing in port, Vincent had Jacob send a messenger with a letter to his son at the Montgomery plantation.

'Lord Pomeroy,

I am a friend of your father's visiting the islands on business. He asked me to deliver something to you. If you would be so kind to come to the Montego Bay Port to the ship *The Fair Wind* at your earliest convenience, I would greatly appreciate it.

Yours respectfully,

Lord McClaren'

Three hours later, Vincent and Jacob were sitting and enjoying the view of the ocean and the quiet of the nearly empty ship. Even though it was only late afternoon, the crew had settled the ship in for the night and Vincent had called an end to the day. The crew, except for the Watch, had gone ashore for an evening off. Davis and Riggs had been sent away as well.

"Excuse me Your Grace," interrupted the roving watchman. "The Watch at the gangplank says a carriage has stopped and a young man is requesting permission to come aboard." He says he is Lord Pomeroy."

Vincent remained seated, nodded to his friend and pulled his wide brimmed hat down lower. "You may allow him aboard."

The roving watchman went to the gangplank and called to the guard below. "You may allow our guest aboard."

Alistair quickly boarded the ship and saw a man approaching him. "Lord Pomeroy, I am Lord McClaren. It is good to meet you," Jacob said giving the young man a nod and extending his hand.

Alistair returned the gesture and shook hands with him. "It is good to meet you as well. You have seen my father? Is he in good health? It seems ever so long since I have seen him."

Jacob nodded. "He is in very good health. He asked me to give you something very special."

Alistair looked expectantly at Jacob, who smiled. "And that would be …?" He was aware of a movement behind Jacob.

"That would be me," said his father moving to stand beside Jacob.

"Father!" cried Alistair grabbing his father and hugging him tightly.

The two men embraced for a moment, then Vincent pushed his son to arm's length and smiled at him. "It is so very good to see you, my son. I was afraid you were angry with me for sending you away. I was afraid you would not see me. Do you forgive me?"

"There is nothing to forgive, Father. You needed time to come to terms with everything. I did as well. I understood that." He looked at his father up and down. "You look very well. I am so glad. I was worried about you." He looked around. "Why didn't you tell me you were coming? Where did you get a ship? This is not one that usually docks here."

"I figured I would arrive before a letter could."

"True enough."

"And the ship is mine. A friend told me to get off my miserable back side and find something to do. I always loved the sea, so I bought a ship. Thought we could do some trade. Oh, my God, Jacob, I am so sorry, this is my son, Alistair. Alistair, this is my friend, Lord McClaren."

"Actually we introduced ourselves," replied Jacob.

"Thank you for encouraging my father to do this."

"Oh, no, not me. I'm just along for the business enterprise."

"Damn, now it my turn to apologize. I want you to meet someone. Come, please, Father." He turned and hurried to the gangplank. Vincent looked at Jacob and shrugged his shoulders and followed his son. Alistair gestured to the open carriage waiting dockside. It was obvious a young lady was waiting there, but as her maid was holding a very large parasol over her, it was impossible to see much of her. "She's most anxious to meet you."

Vincent looked down at himself. He and Jacob had left their coats in their cabins due to the heat. He was not even wearing a cravat. They hadn't expected to see anyone but Alistair. "I am not properly attired to meet a young lady."

Alistair laughed. "No one thinks too much of that here. We do follow the rules of propriety when going out, but dress much cooler at home. The ship is your home for the present, she will think nothing of it." He started on down the gangplank, followed reluctantly by this father.

As they arrived at the carriage, Alistair said, "Father, may I present Miss Gabriella Montegue, Mrs. Montgomery's niece. Gabriella, this is my father, His Grace, the Duke of Edgingham."

The young lady inclined her head and held out her hand. Vincent took it and kissed it and said, "I am most please to meet a friend of my son. Please forgive my appearance, we did not expect such charming company this evening." He released her hand and assessed the young lady. She was very petite with pale skin, dark brown hair and laughing brown eyes.

"My Lord Duke, it is of no consequence. We are quite used to the heat. I am sure it is quite a transition for you from your lovely cool England. You must come stay at the plantation. The Great House was built for this climate and is quite cool. I am sure my aunt and uncle would insist that you should join us if they were here. My aunt loves company since she does not travel about much unless she absolutely must. My uncle would love to see you, I am sure. He is very busy with the plantation right now and does not get out much either."

Vincent laughed. "That is most generous of you, but I am here with friends. I could not possible abandon them."

She laughed. "That is not a problem, Your Grace. They are most welcome. The house is quite large and can accommodate many guests. You will all be much more comfortable at the Great House."

He looked at his son. Alistair added, "Please Father, we will be able to spend more time together."

"Very well, but I cannot possibly come at this moment. I will see if Lord McClaren wishes to join us. If you could call for us tomorrow? If Lord McClaren joins us, that will be three of us and I have two servants."

Alistair immediately replied, "I will be here early in the morning. We are only about an hour away. You will enjoy the journey, the view is beautiful all the way."

"Please, join us on deck. I will order tea."

Alistair offered his hand to help Gabriella down. "I would enjoy something to drink, but we cannot stay too long. It is unwise to travel too late in the day."

Vincent had noticed several outriders waiting several paces back. "Of course, I will send drinks to your men as well." He escorted his son and the young lady on board the ship, followed by her maid. The woman stood close to Gabriella holding the umbrella over her charge.

An hour later, Vincent walked his son and guest back to their carriage. He once again kissed Gabriella's hand, then patted his son on the shoulder. "I will look forward to seeing you in the morning."

Alistair hugged his father again, "I am so glad you are doing well. I have so much to tell you. I am anxious for morning." He climbed into the carriage and they were off, waving their goodbyes.

Vincent, however, was feeling very uneasy. Gabriella's maid gave him a very strange feeling. Lady's maids were supposed to be imposing to protect their young charges, but this one was very different. He didn't like it.

Chapter Eleven: The Plantation

True to his word, an hour after the sun was up, Alistair arrived with a closed carriage and a cart. Vincent and Jacob had already planned their strategy. Jacob and Angus would stay with the ship. They felt it would give them more freedom to do their business. Vincent would spend time with his son, gaining as much knowledge of the plantations as he could. Jacob and Angus would be looking at the trade side of sugar. They would all be showing interest in getting involved in making money with sugar, all the while keeping their ears open for any problems for the government.

It did not take them long to get loaded and on the road to the Montgomery Plantation. On the way, they could see people working in the fields. "It is harvest time for the sugarcane. These slaves are cutting the cane and then it will be brought to the mills to be made into sugar. It is quite a process," Alistair told his father.

"I would very much like to see that. I can not imagine how these green plants get turned into grains of sugar," remarked Vincent.

Alistair frowned and waited until they were on a stretch of road with no one near and said very softly so the driver could not hear him, "But here they use slaves to do all the work. Some of the landowners do not treat them very well, some are downright cruel. I am pleased to say that Mr. Montgomery takes good care of his people. He realizes he could not run the plantation without them, so he takes care of them. Some of the landowners consider them expendable and are only concerned with their productivity."

His father replied, "I am sure that creates some considerable problems. Unhappy people cause trouble."

"It is something to be very careful about discussing around others. Most of the landowners do not appreciate criticism. Mr. Montgomery is not always popular with his peers as he is rather outspoken on the subject."

Vincent asked, "Yesterday, you mentioned that it wasn't safe to be out too late. I see that once again you have outriders. Is robbery a great possibility here?"

Alistair was quiet for a minute, then replied, "There is unrest not only among the slaves, but the Maroons as well, that is what the locals are called. They are also unhappy with British rule. Most of the owners keep their plantations well-fortified. The soldiers here keep things under control, but Mr. Montgomery says there aren't enough of them if things get out of hand. The government on the island tries to keep this quiet. Mr. Montgomery's people are not afraid of him, they talk to him. They are afraid of trouble from the Maroons."

"Very well, let's talk of nicer things." They had been speaking softly, but now he said in a louder voice, "Tell me about Mademoiselle Montegue." He laughed as his son blushed.

"She is a beautiful woman. When I am with her, I can think of nothing else. However, I am not sure I am ready for marriage. So much I want to see and do. I would value your input, Father."

Vincent smiled. "Give me some time to get to know her, but ultimately that is a decision only you can make. Be sure to take your time. Be sure of your answer to your own question."

Alistair spent the rest of the ride describing the countryside, telling his father who owned what and what the land was used for. As they climbed the hills, they would occasionally get beautiful glimpses of the ocean. The ride did not seem that long when they arrived at the Montgomery Great House.

They met Mr. Montgomery returning from his morning ride. He rode alongside them up the drive to the house. He dismounted, tossed the reins to a boy and approached the carriage. He approached Vincent. "Your Grace, it has been such a long time since we have met. Ten years, I believe, since I was in England."

Vincent extended his hand. "Mr. Montgomery, please call me Vincent. It is good to see you again. I appreciate the courtesy you have extended my son. I believe travel and new adventures are necessary to become a well-rounded gentleman."

"I would be honored, Vincent, then you must call me Paul. Alistair has been a delight to have. Come, let us get inside before the heat gets to be too much. The house was built to keep as cool as possible in this tropical paradise." He led them into the house. "Would you like to refresh yourself in your rooms, or would you like a cool drink on the veranda? It is quite nice there almost any time of day."

"I believe I would like to freshen up first," replied Vincent.

"Lazlo?" Paul called to his butler. "Show His Grace to his room. Oh, and Vincent, feel free to leave your coat. We dress casually here in the house."

Vincent did not wait long before he was joined by Riggs and Davis. As soon as they arrived, they started looking carefully around the room for any spy holes as was their habit, while His Grace began making a lot of noise as he washed and changed his shirt and cravat. Riggs found one behind a picture. Vincent found this very disconcerting.

"Riggs, I am going to need cooler clothes here. See what you can do. I am officially out of mourning so the light colors they wear will be appropriate. Davis, tell the butler, what is his name?"

"Lazlo, Your Grace."

"Yes, Lazlo, tell him that I have placed you in his service while here." He hesitated, made sure his back was to the painting and winked at Davis. "Tell him I won't have you lazing about with nothing to do. Now be off with you. I do expect you to report in every evening, so I can keep up with you."

Davis was standing so that His Grace blocked the view from the painting. He smirked as he bowed. "Of course, Your Grace." He turned and left.

"Do you know which room is my son's? I would like to see him before I go downstairs."

"I believe Lord Alistair did not come upstairs, but went in search of the young lady, Your Grace."

"Hmmmm." He took a final look in the mirror. "Very well, then if you are done with me, I guess I shall join the others."

Riggs bowed his head in agreement. "Of course, Your Grace."

Chapter Twelve: Gabriella

Vincent sat on his balcony enjoying the cooler late night air. He had removed the jacket he had worn to dinner and thrown it on the bed. The people here had acclimatized and claimed the house quite cool. He, however, with his English blood found the house very warm. Even the lighter weight clothes Lazlo had sent up with Riggs didn't help that much. The balcony offered a breeze which helped.

He had found the evening quite tedious. He had been very unsure if he could pull off the fop character with his son around, but actually it had been quite easy. Alistair paid very little attention to his father all evening. He was enamored with Gabriella and she was obviously keeping his attention centered on her. She had been quite charming, but he still had a very uneasy feeling about her.

Paul had invited him to go along on his morning ride and promised a look at the sugar production. It would just be the two of them as Paul had assigned his son, Paul Lucian and Alistair to check on the cane gathering. His thoughts were interrupted by Riggs entering quietly. "It's all right, Riggs, you don't have to be quiet."

"So sorry to disturb you, Your Grace. I know you like your privacy, but a letter just came from Lord McClaren. Being so late and all, I figured it was important."

Vincent rose and entered his bed chamber. He took the envelope and moved near the lamp on the desk. There were actually two letters in it. He read the one from Jacob first.

'Vincent

John Ayscough, acting governor, already knows of our arrival. He requests an audience at your convenience. I received an invitation as well. As I am only the son of a Duke, I shall let you deal with this. Of course, I shall do what you think best.

Regards

Jacob'

Vincent sighed and opened the other letter.

'Your Grace,

We are truly honored that you and Lord McClaren have chosen to visit us on our little island. I humbly request an audience, at your convenience of course. I would love fresh news from home and would like the privilege of sharing some insights on our government here for you to share with our King. Perhaps you would allow me to give a fete in your honor so our friends could have the privilege of meeting you both.

Your servant,

John Ayscough, Governor of Jamaica'

Vincent shuddered at the thought of a fete in his honor. "Tell the messenger I have retired for the evening and you may not disturb me. Lazlo can decide to put him up for the night or send him on his way. I'll deal with this tomorrow."

"Of course, Your Grace."

As was his habit, Vincent awoke before the sun rose. Riggs was accustomed to this and was already setting up things for him to prepare for the day. He handed him his tea and said, "Good morning, Your Grace. I trust you slept well."

"Not really. It is too warm here. I am to go riding with Montgomery this morning."

"Yes, I know. Lazlo gave me clothes for you to wear. Apparently they don't wear coats much here. I was just given breeches, a loose fitting sort of shirt, and a wide brimmed hat and told it was proper attire to go out this morning. I hope you will approve."

"That would create quite a sensation at home, but when in Rome as they say." He allowed Riggs to help him dress as who knew who might be

77

watching. He had to admit, the clothes were cooler, but still felt very strange to be so, so undressed.

"Mr. Montgomery left word that he would await you in his office."

Vincent found Paul at his desk going over some papers. "Ah, good, you are up. Ready to see how sugar is made?"

"Yes, sounds interesting."

"It's a hot, grubby process, so we need to see it early before the day gets to be too hot. I change out the workers every hour. Most planters don't, but I find them too valuable to let them die so easily. A little caution saves them, good for them, good for me. Once the cane is ready, we are on a tight time schedule. Cane must be crushed for the juice within 24 hours of cutting it. The mill works day and night till the job is done. You will see how it works." He rose from his desk and took a large brimmed hat off the hat rack near the door. "You had a messenger last night. I had Lazlo put him up for the night. Do you need to respond?"

"Yes, but I have not decided what to say yet. The governor wants to see me."

"Hmphf. He would. Probably wants to complain about lack of military help here. The Maroons are always causing trouble. They don't want us here."

"I see. I know I must see him, represent the King and all that, just not in a hurry to do it."

"We can talk about that later. Our horses should be ready. The mill is on the other side of the slave quarters."

As the rode up, he could see four oxen, each circling a strange machine with rollers. Slaves were feeding the cane into the rollers, which crushed out the juice and it ran down into large containers. When they were full, men would carry them over to the fire pits. It was very noisy in the grinding area. Paul motioned and they rode over to the boiling area. He still had to yell to be heard. "The cane is crushed, then the juice is brought over here and put in the large pot on the end. You see we use the crushed cane plants, called bagasse, to fuel the fire. We add lime to the juice to help settle out the impurities, which settle to the bottom of the kettle. The scum that rises to the top gets taken off and can be fed to our cattle, as well as the impurities on the bottom. We try to use it all and not waste. As it cooks down, it is poured into a smaller pot, and so on down the line."

"So you let it boil dry, is that when the sugar is left?"

"No, you see that woman taking some juice out of the teache, that last pot. She is the judge of whether it is ready or not. Only experience can judge from sight and sound of the boiling juice if it is ready. She will take out a small sample to test, then decide when it is done. Then the syrup is poured into a cooling trough. The gur or solid sugar is shoveled into those hogsheads over there, taken to the curing house and allowed to set. The molasses will be poured into other kegs. Some of the molasses will go over to the distillery to be made into rum."

"My goodness, that is hot, dirty work. I don't think I could even deal with your job. This heat is just too much for me."

Paul smiled. "I've lived here all my life. I am quite used to it. My father started this plantation and I hope Paul Lucian will continue the tradition. I believe he will. Let us go toward the fields, it is cooler there."

It didn't take them long to be out in one of the fields. Paul had chosen one with no workers, but they could see the slaves working in a distant field, men, women, children, all busy. Paul stopped his horse and Vincent did the same. Paul said, "I wanted to speak to you privately. I hope anything I say will be kept confidential."

"Of course, is everything all right?"

"I am fine with my lot in life. I have my home, my son. I am concerned about Alistair. I feel he is very enamored with Gabriella. I feel this is not a good thing. All is not what it seems with her.

Margarite quite dotes on her niece. I do not approve, but it is my wife's money that controls our destiny. Margarite's family is very intertwined with the religion of this area. It is called Obeah. Publicly she professes to be Catholic, but her maid and Gabriella's are practitioners of Obeah and through it they influence Margarite and Gabriella. I am sure Gabriella's maid, Delyse, has decided her charge will be the next Duchess of Edgingham. I really do not think you want that to happen. You must get Alistair away from here. I am sure Delyse has put some spell on him. As you saw last night, when he is around my niece, he sees nothing else. Please excuse any intrusion on my part, I only feel concern for your family."

"I understand. Thank you for the warning. I think now I have an answer for that messenger. May I borrow a carriage? I will send it back upon our arrival in Kingston."

"Of course, what ever you need, Your Grace."

They rode through a couple fields, Paul discussing the sugar cane and the requirements for growing it. Upon his return to the house, Vincent sent for Riggs. He immediately penned a response to both Jacob and the governor.

'Governor Ayscough,

Lord McClaren, Lord Pomeroy, and I would be most happy to meet with you on Monday afternoon for tea if that would be convenient. I find myself quite unwell due to the heat here in Jamaica, therefore I request it be a private affair.

Sincerely,

Pomeroy, Duke of Edgingham'

His letter to Jacob was less formal.

'Jacob,

I hope you can conclude your business quickly. I need to get my son off this island. The enclosed is a reply to the Governor for tea on Monday. I want to leave as soon as possible after that. Alistair and I will be joining you later today.

Vincent'

He put those letters in one envelope and addressed it to Jacob. Then he quickly wrote another letter and addressed it. He gave the letter for Jacob to Riggs. "Please tell the messenger to deliver this to Lord McClaren as soon as possible." Then he handed him the other letter. "Tell him I want this on the first ship headed east. Then find Davis and ask him to help Alistair pack his things. The Governor has requested our presence and we really shouldn't keep him waiting. I want to leave as soon after breakfast as Alistair can be ready."

Riggs looked directly at Vincent and mouthed, 'Permanently'. Vincent merely nodded.

He hurried down to breakfast. He was not at all surprised to see Gabriella already sitting beside Alistair monopolizing his attention. He went to the sideboard and helped himself to the whiting, eggs, a good helping of fruit and toast. He chose the seat beside his son. A footman approached and asked, "What would you like to drink, Your Grace. We have coffee, tea, juice, milk, cocoa."

"I believe I would like tea, thank you."

"Father, you should really try this chocolate coffee that Gabriella likes. It is quite tasty."

Vincent found himself loathe to try anything Gabriella recommended since his talk with Paul, so he politely said, "This heat is making me feel quite unwell, I think I will stay with the familiar for now. Thank you."

He took a couple bites of his fish. "I am afraid I have rather distressing news. The Governor has requested a meeting with us. We should handle this post haste."

"Us? Why would the Governor want to see me? I can understand why he would want to see you, but me?" Alistair looked puzzled.

"You are my son and heir. This is a good opportunity for you to see Affairs of State in action. You must learn that in our position, we represent our King and country no matter where we go. You will have to do this one of these days, you should learn how to do it now, while I am around to show you."

"When do you have to go?" asked Gabriella. "Surely the Governor is going to give you a big party. You are such an important person. Can't we all go, Uncle? It would be such fun."

"You know I can not leave now. The sugar mill is critical right now," responded Paul.

"I have declined any parties, it will be just a meeting with the Governor."

Gabriella looked quite put out. She turned to Alistair and said, clearly pouting, "But I do not want you to leave. You must stay. Your father can take care of this himself, can he not?"

Vincent's temper was rising, but he managed to say quietly, "I need my son with me. He must learn his position." Gabriella looked about to say something.

Paul looked at his niece, "Gabriella, that is enough. We can not invite ourselves to the Governors. If you cannot be quiet, you may leave the table."

"You will come back, will you not?"

"Of course I will. Do not fret. We should only be gone a couple of days." He smiled at her and patted her hand.

"I suggest you finish your breakfast and go pack your things," replied his father. "Davis is available to help you. He knows what you will need. I want to leave as soon as you are ready. I want to get this over and done with."

Chapter Thirteen: The Governor

Two hours later they were on the way back to Kingston in the closed traveling carriage with their luggage strapped to the top and back. Vincent chose to ignore his son's sullen attitude. "I am quite sure the Governor wants to discuss with us the situation here with the natives. It will be a very tiresome meeting. These things always are," Vincent remarked fanning himself with a palmleaf fan. "The most important thing to do is listen and not make any commitments. It is not our place to speak for the King unless he specifically asks us to. I try to avoid that situation. We are usually required to attend numerous social affairs, but I am begging off, using my illness with the heat as my excuse."

"Father, I am very concerned about you. You haven't seemed yourself since you arrived."

"I am quite fine." He looked at Riggs, who raised an eyebrow, then looked quickly out the window. Davis appeared quite engrossed with the view out his window. "We have much to discuss when we arrive in Kingston. We shall stay aboard the ship while there. I prefer its privacy to pubic inns. We certainly will not be staying at the Governor's." They spent the rest of the ride into town in silence.

Upon arriving at the ship, they were met by Jacob. "I have a cabin all ready for Alistair."

Vincent replied. "Thank you, Jacob. Alistair, why don't you go get settled, I need to discuss some things with Lord McClaren? Jacob, if you could come to my cabin? Davis, would you see that our things are brought aboard, and the carriage is returned to Mr. Montgomery?"

It didn't take Vincent long to fill Jacob up on what all had happened at the plantation. "Therefore, my son will be leaving with us even though he does not know that at this moment. Please see that he does not leave the ship without me. I will inform him it is not safe to do so, but he is quite enamored with the young lady."

"Understood. As to what we have learned, it is much the same as you already know. The Maroons have a safe place up in the hills, but they cause trouble whenever they can. The King has sent some soldiers to reinforce the situation here, but not enough. I am sure the Governor will be requesting more."

Vincent nodded. "Nothing I can do about that but report it to our benefactor who will report it to the King. What they will do I have no idea."

The next afternoon, a carriage Jacob had rented for them arrived promptly at a quarter to four and took them to the Governor's residence. What

Vincent had hoped to be a small intimate affair, turned out to be a rather large gathering of approximately a hundred people. Fortunately, it was set up in the very large and beautiful garden where the breeze from the ocean helped to maintain a cooler temperature. "We are so delighted with your presence, My Lord Duke. So many of our British subjects wished to meet you. I do hope you do not object. Once people knew you were here, they were so insistent. We so seldom receive such august personages to our small island. And to have three members of the peerage here, Your Grace, Lord McClaren and Lord Pomeroy, well, I just could not refuse them," simpered Governor Ayscough.

Vincent would have loved to have turned and fled, but knew that he could not. He endured a rather long receiving line. Once the last person had moved on, he turned to the Governor. "Governor, I must apologize, but the crush of people is overwhelming, therefore if you wish to have a private word, I would suggest you do so immediately. I feel quite faint from this heat."

"Oh, of course, My Lord Duke, let us adjourn to my private office which is just over here. I have doors directly from my office to the gardens. I do so love the view." They entered the office and left the large double glass paned doors open. Guards were stationed to keep people at bay so their conversation could be private.

"Please, My Lord Duke, be seated, have something cool to drink." He waved in a footman with a tray of cool drinks.

Vincent seated himself and the others did as well. He looked at the proffered tray of drinks. "And what are these?"

The footman replied, "The tall glasses are Planter's punch, a rum drink. The short glasses are Sangaree, a wine drink, My Lord Duke." Vincent chose a punch, while Alistair took the Sangaree. Jacob, also, took a punch.

"I do hope you will get right to the point, Governor." He took a sip of his punch.

"Of course, My Lord Duke. The natives, called Maroons are becoming a large problem. I firmly believe they want to take their island back. I do not have enough soldiers here to prevent that. I need help."

Vincent sighed. "I assumed that is what you wished to tell me. I fear there is nothing I can do except let the King know. I am sure you have already done so." He picked up a fan off the little table near his chair and proceeded to use it vigorously. "If that is all you have to say, I would really like to leave now. The heat is making me feel quite unwell."

Jacob added, "We are merely here on business. We may be peers of the realm, but we have no control on what the King decides. We can send him a message, but …"

The Governor looked stricken, "But you are a Duke! You have power! Surely your requests get results!"

Vincent laughed. "The King does not answer to me, I answer to the King. If you wish to send a letter with us, I will see that His Majesty gets it. Other than that, I can not help you. I do not have his ear. Alistair, please go request our carriage. I must go and lie down." Alistair hurried from the room. He took another sip of his drink. "That is really quite good, you must send me a copy of the recipe." With 7that he rose and headed out the door through the house to the exit and awaited his carriage.

Jacob hesitated until Vincent and Alistair were out of hearing, then he turned to the Governor and said quietly, "I would send that letter to the ship by tonight." Then he followed them out of the building.

As they entered the carriage, Alistair asked, "Now may I return to the Mongomerys?"

"You will spend the night," replied his father.

Chapter Fourteen: Alistair

Alistair awoke to strange sounds. It was daylight. He looked out his porthole and all he could see was the ocean. He quickly dressed and hurried up on deck. He looked around him in shock. They were at sea. Jamaica was well behind them. He saw his father on the bridge with Lord McClaren and the helmsman. He hurried up to join them. His father finished speaking to Lord McClaren, who then turned and said to the helmsman, "Tie it off, and leave the bridge. He followed the man off.

"Good morning, Alistair."

"Father, what are you doing? Why have we left Jamaica?"

"Jamaica is a dangerous place. They are in a state of rebellion. It is not a place for us."

"But I wanted to return to the Montgomerys. I promised Gabreilla."

His father nodded. "Yes, another dangerous situation. Mr. Montgomery warned me that Gabreilla had her hooks in you. Not a wise alliance."

"But Father!"

"Alistair, you are going to be the next Duke of Edgingham. You must choose your wife carefully. Money is not really important, we have plenty, but breeding is. Miss Montegue has neither. You are merely enamored because her maid is using her Obeah powers to attach you to the young lady. Now that you are away from that, you will soon find her charms less enthralling."

Alistair was stunned. He walked to the railing and looked out over the sea. "Father, I am very confused. So much I do not understand. We always were so close, then Mother was killed, and you withdrew from everyone. You sent me away. And now … well now, you have changed. You do not seem yourself. I don't know what to think. I thought I had found my place in the world, and then you arrive, and it is all confused again."

Vincent walked over and put his hand on his son's shoulder. "Let us retire to my cabin where we can talk in comfort." He turned his son, put his arm around his shoulder and they went to the cabin. On the way, he called to Riggs, "Tell Ilya, breakfast for two in my cabin, please."

Arriving there, he removed his coat and hat and threw them on the bed and took a chair and indicated for Alistair to do so as well. "Your mother was the light of my life. Losing her sent me to a very dark place and I didn't want to drag you there as well. When I was your age, I was at sea, I did not take the Grand Tour. Most young men of

92

our station in life take the Grand Tour, to educate themselves of the world, my brothers did. I decided that is what I needed to do with you. You needed to be free to grow, not chained to my misery. I am sorry if that was the wrong decision."

"That is both a yes and a no. I felt it was wrong because I wanted to stay with you, to be there for you, to comfort you and be comforted by you. On the other hand, Mr. Harris, the escort you sent with me, explained that traveling was what young men of my station did to increase their education of the world. He said you probably needed time to come to terms with what had happened. It did make sense to me and after I time, I overcame my distress about it. When I met up with Paul Lucian and we had finished touring Europe, he invited me home with him. Mr. Harris declined and returned home. I had planned to stay in Jamaica for awhile and then maybe go to Uncle Quinten."

"An excellent idea, I think you should do that."

"But now I have you again. Why can I not stay with you?"

"My life is very complicated now. What I am about to tell you stays only with us, do you understand? There is much in life you will learn you must keep to yourself. This is one of those things. Not to anyone, not to Uncle Quinten, no one. Jacob will know that you are aware, but no one else."

93

"Father, I don't understand."

"Just promise me."

"Of course, you taught me when quite young not to tell anything I knew to others."

Vincent smiled at him. There was a knock at the door. "Enter." Ilya brought in their breakfast, served them and left them alone again.

"I had allowed the world to think I had become a drunken sot and isolated myself in the country. I had not. It wasn't easy. I wanted to, but I remembered that my grandfather had been one and almost lost everything we had. I didn't want to do that. I did allow myself an occasional evening of oblivion, but only occasionally. Lord Peters came to see me and told me to get off my duff and be useful." He smiled at the look on his son's face.

"Lord Peters? He's a spy. Everyone knows that. What did he want with you?"

"Lord Peters is not a spy. People think he is a spy because he runs that department of the government. He gets people like me to do his spying." He laughed as that thought settled into Alistair's head."

"You? You are a spy? But you've become a … a …"

Vincent laughed again. "A fop? A dandy? I did not think you had noticed. Yes, a very useful tool. People do not suspect me of anything."

Alistair was still incredulous. "But you are a Duke, a gentleman, what do you know of such things?"

Vincent roared with laughter. "I have not always been thus. You know before your grandfather died, I was a Captain in His Majesty's Navy. I have done many things of ungentlemanly caliber. I just have not talked about that part of my life. The sea is a rough life. I have sheltered you from that part of my history, but that's where I met Jacob. You know that Riggs, Jamison, Davis were with me during those times. They were a part of my crew then and are a part of my crew now. This ship is a safe place. We can be ourselves here. But I want you to have no part in this. I have raised you to be the next Duke of Edgingham."

"No! I want to be a part of this. That is so exciting. I want to share this with you."

"No. It is very dangerous. You are my only heir. I will not have you involved. Life is dangerous enough without being involved in this. I am taking you to Uncle Quinten. I sent him a letter before I left England that I would hope to meet up with him in the Azores within the month. I recently sent him another to Graciosa, hoping he will be there."

"Father, I have to say, you are constantly a surprise to me."

"Good. Let that be a lesson for you. Keep yourself to yourself. Do not let just anyone know the real you."

A month later they arrived at Graciosa in the Azores. The winds had not always been kind to them. Quinten arrived a couple days later, and they spent a week enjoying the beauty of the islands and their family reunion. He was delighted to take his nephew under his wing. He was working with the East India Company and assured both Alistair and Vincent he would make the boy rich. He wanted Vincent to join them and come to India where he was now living, but Vincent had been far from home long enough.

Two weeks later, they sailed into London, leaving Davis to deliver reports to their benefactor. Another day's sail delivered Jacob and Angus back to Scotland. Vincent declined the invitation to spend a few days as he was anxious to return home for a rest. He knew his men were anxious to be home as well. He was quite sure that when Davis returned, he would have another mission for them.

Chapter Fifteen: A New Problem

Vincent took the slouch hat from Riggs, put it on and looked in the mirror. Yes, that would do. He was sure he had not met the lady, but that didn't mean she didn't know him. He nodded. He looked like the lads who worked in the stables. "Thank you, Riggs. You may retire. I have no idea how late they will arrive. Please do not wait up for me."

"Very well, Your Grace."

Vincent went to his office, removed the hat and stood looking out the window while he contemplated. He was tired, not just from his trip, he had arrived home just two days ago. He was quite sure he was ready to retire, again. He had been doing missions for the Home Office for fifteen years. He was sixty years old. People his age and station did not work. Granted he was in much better condition than his contemporaries, and it had been fun. He had to admit that. Plus it had kept him in good condition.

He had thought about it all the way home from India. He had taken several missions there and had enjoyed his time with Alistair and his family. Soon after arriving in India, his son had met a lovely English girl and married her. They now had four children. Thinking of his grandchildren brought a smile to his lips. Quinten had retired and wanted him to come retire with him in India where it was sunny and warm. That wouldn't do for him. He did not like the heat, besides Alistair and his family would be moving back to England next year to put young Vincent Alistair in school at Eton.

As to those here at home, The Jamisons had retired two years hence. The maid, Tessie, had turned out to be quite a surprise. She had been such a silly goose when first employed, but she was smart and learned quickly. She had become quite a rock in their household. She and Davis had married and were now in charge of the household, he as butler and she as housekeeper. Riggs, bless him, was having problems with his health. He should really retire him, as well, but was not sure who could step in. Riggs swore he would never retire, he needed to be busy. He sighed. Many things to consider.

He turned to his desk and picked up a bag of coins and the hat. He would go play cards with the lads. It was a treat for them, a way to thank them for all their hard work that his missions caused them. He always let them win some extra money. They knew he lost to them on purpose, but it was still great fun.

He walked slowly to the barn. Yes, he was ready to retire. He would talk to Jacob, give it all to him. He had not seen Jacob in several months as Jacob had taken some missions in the colonies and Canada. The young men, Will and Ben, Jacob had recruited, had turned out very well. Jacob, therefore had his own team and between them, they had handled more ventures. They had arrived back in London a week ago, therefore they had taken this job. Seemed like they were always traveling, England was spreading into so many parts of the world.

It was around two in the morning when the group entered, and the heavy doors closed. Jacob pulled the hood off the woman and dismounted, then he helped her dismount. Vincent moved to help with the horses. Jacob led their guest over to a stall that was fitted with a nice mound of hay covered with a blanket and a large box on which was set up dishes, food, and a couple bottles of wine. "Have a seat. They left us a picnic. We have to care for the horses. Go ahead and eat something. I insist. We have a long way to go yet. We will rest here for a few hours." He opened a bottle so she could pour herself some wine. Jacob left her and moved to help settle the horses.

Vincent moved to Jacob's side. They spoke only of their work until they were sure she was asleep. "Good to see you again, my friend. It's been a long time," Vincent finally remarked.

"We have been rather busy and in different directions. Good to see you too."

"After this, we need to take some time off and catch up." Jacob nodded. "How did this one go?" asked Vincent.

"Extremely well. I think I could have talked her into coming of her own free will from the first, but her son interfered, so we had to wait until dark and steal her from his residence. She was no trouble and came willingly. Lady Tremayne is a gutsy lady." Jacob smiled at his last comment.

"Does she have any idea what her husband was up to?"

"No, none," replied Jacob, shaking his head. "She says he didn't discuss his business with her, but she doesn't think he had any dealings with her father."

"Well, we've been asked to find out, so do what you can. We must protect her at all costs. From everything I have learned about them, she is not guilty of anything. Her husband and son probably are. I will have to deal with her son at some time. Keep me apprised of anything you learn. You can use the pigeons, or if necessary, send the yacht. I have already written a friend in the colonies to see what he can learn of her father." Vincent left the barn in the capable hands of his men and Jacob's.

A little over a week later, he received a letter from Jacob by special messenger. "Discussed subject with my guest. Her son was furious that he found nothing on the subject. Insisted he knew everything about their business. She knows nothing. She would not know if he had communicated with her father. I believe we need to get the word out that there isn't a new weapon. She won't be safe as long as this rumor is out there."

Vincent contemplated that for awhile. Official agents had interrogated her son, Wyn. The office had been searched thoroughly, much to Wyn's displeasure. From the sounds of things, Westminster needed to look inside its own house for the solution to the problem. Sounded to him like the spy was there, but he felt he had to find out some things for himself.

Chapter Sixteen: Tremayne

Two weeks later, Pomeroy's large traveling coach with eight outriders fully outfitted in His Grace's livery pulled up outside Tremayne's country estate early in the afternoon. Davis climbed down from the back of the coach and opened the door. Riggs stepped out and went to the door and knocked. The butler opened the door and was appropriately awestruck. "His Grace, the Duke of Edgingham to see Lord Tremayne," announced Riggs handing him a card.

Stunned, it took the man a moment to answer. "I will announce His Grace immediately. Would he like to wait in the Drawing Room and I will order some refreshments, or would he prefer to freshen up?"

Riggs looked at the butler like he was an idiot. "Of course His Grace would like to freshen up. It is a long journey from his estate." Riggs turned and nodded toward Davis, who assisted His Grace from the coach. Then both he and Riggs got in the coach to be driven to the servants' entrance around back.

The butler had rung for a maid. "Take His Grace to the Rose Suite and get him anything he needs." He immediately went in search of Lord Tremayne.

She showed him up the stairs to a large suite. "Is there anything I can bring you, Your Grace?"

"Just send my valet to me. He can tell you what is required." She curtsied and left. She returned within a few minutes with a pitcher of hot water, fresh towels and Riggs. Vincent took his time 'refreshing' himself. It didn't take long to wash up and have Riggs brush off his clothes and tie a fresh cravat, so he mostly sat reading a book he had brought. The men discussed nothing except what was necessary to 'refresh' oneself, as one never knew who might be listening. Vincent knew that Tremayne would fall over himself to rush to the Drawing Room as soon as he heard a Duke had arrived to see him, so he decided that he would make him wait, make him nervous. Finally after an hour, he rose from the settee, nodded to Riggs who rang for a maid. When she arrived, Vincent said, "I think I feel refreshed enough to see His Lordship."

She curtsied and replied, "If you will follow me." He followed her down the stairs where he was then led by the butler to the Drawing Room. As Vincent entered the Drawing Room, Cessily Tremayne immediately stood and made an elaborate curtsy. Wyn was pacing around and stopped and bowed appropriately. "Your Grace, we are very pleased by your visit. Please be seated." He waved Vincent toward a large comfortable chair.

Vincent gave them each a nod. "Thank you for your hospitality, Lord and Lady Tremayne."

Wyn replied, "Please call me Wyn. We are delighted to have you visit."

"I've ordered tea. It should be arriving shortly," responded Cessily.

Vincent fanned himself with his handkerchief and sounded flustered. "Oh, that would be just lovely, the trip seemed ever so long, but I decided I really must come myself rather than send my business manager. I thought it too important to trust anyone else with this discussion, but it can wait until after tea. I am quite parched and have to admit, hungry as well. My cook did pack us a picnic basket as I find inn food unpalatable; but eating in the coach is so messy and stopping along the way is just too rustic. I just do not abide picnics, one's clothes get wrinkled and dusty, and then there are the insects." He made a face. Then he smiled at Cessily. "You look quite lovely, my dear. It is so refreshing to find a fashionably dressed lady in the country. I find so many ladies let themselves go when they retire to the country."

"Why thank you, Your Grace. I recently returned from a shopping trip to Paris. Wyn had to go on business and I took the opportunity to go shopping."

"Oh, Paris! I love shopping in Paris. So much more variety than in London. We British are so stuffy about our style. Paris is so refreshingly modern."

At that moment the butler arrived with two footmen and laid out tea on the low table in front of them. Conversation turned to tea and food until the servants exited the room. Cessily poured tea for them all and fixed a plate of sandwiches, finger foods, and biscuits and handed it to Vincent, then one for Wyn and a small one for herself. Wyn ignored his and just had tea. Vincent nibbled a bite or two off of everything while they chatted about London gossip, the area, the weather, mundane things one discussed at tea with ladies. He managed to draw tea out to almost an hour, knowing Wyn was bursting to know the real reason for his visit.

Finally, he said, "Well, I really do hate to rush along, but I would like a private word, please, Wyn. I really must be leaving soon, I do hope you don't mind, Lady Tremayne."

"Oh, no, of course not. I am most delighted that you spent some time bringing me up to date on London news. I will leave you gentlemen to your discussions. Please have a safe journey." With that she left the room, being sure to close the door behind her.

"So, Your Grace, how can I be of service to you?"

"I will not beat around the proverbial bush and be quite blunt, a rumor has reached me that your father had some new weapon invention and needed backers. I know some time has passed, but I have been indisposed. However, I don't wish to be left out. I am always interested in making money, who isn't? However, like some of my peers, I am not afraid of new ideas. I can be very discreet, I am so interested." He was watching Wyn's face intently as he spoke. His expression had been curious and interested until Vincent mentioned the invention, then it turned momentarily wary, then dark.

"I am afraid you have been misinformed, Your Grace." He hadn't missed that Pomeroy had not given him permission to call him by his Christian name. "I have heard those rumors as well, but I assure you they are quite untrue. If my father had any new ideas, he did not make any record of them. I have been fully involved in our family's business since I became of age, and Father told me nothing about any new idea. Westminster has been rather difficult about it, but I keep assuring them there is nothing. I even went so far as to recently go to Paris myself to see if he had contacted anyone there, but he had not. We are loyal British subjects. My family would never betray our country."

Vincent immediately looked shocked and flustered. "Oh my goodness, Westminster didn't accuse you of that, did they?"

"They did insinuate that possibility. They seemed to think if he couldn't get funding from them, he would go elsewhere. I was quite devastated. I looked into it myself. I am quite sure he did not go elsewhere."

"Oh you poor thing! What a trial this must have been! And then here I come, bringing it all up again. My deepest apologies. I am quite shaken to have caused you any distress. I am sure you are quite done with me. If you will send for my coach and servants, I will leave you to your peace. I am so sorry to have disturbed you. Please forgive me."

"It is quite all right, Your Grace. You had no way of knowing. Please don't feel the need to hurry away. You are quite welcome to stay and rest from your journey. We would love to have you dine with us this evening, stop here to break your journey." Wyn rang for a maid. However, it wasn't one of his maids who arrived, but Riggs and Davis.

His Grace continued to sit comfortably in his chair. "I am afraid I am not sure I believe you. I am very loyal to King and country. I want to be very sure you are too. I, also, want to be very sure you aren't holding anything back. I do so hate that. Mr. Riggs is very good at getting the truth out of people. Mr. Davis will assist him. I, myself, find myself quite faint at the sight of blood, so I will leave you in their capable hands."

He rose from his chair. Tremayne was frozen with shock. Davis and Riggs moved to stand on either side of him. "Oh, and before you get any ideas of hope for a rescue, my men are holding your staff hostage in the kitchen. No one is going to help you." He started for the door. "Oh, and one more thing. You can babble all you like to people about this later, no one will believe you. You are a nobody within the Ton, where I … well, we both know who I am. No one will believe anything you say about this. It's a good way to end up in Bedlam. Well, I shall be in the room you so generously set up for me. Call me when you are ready to talk."

"Wait, please. Wait, I … I …"

Vincent turned, holding up his monocle and looking at Tremayne. "Yes, you have something to say. Please don't bore me with nonsense. I am already late to a house party."

"I looked, I really searched everything. All I found was a note in my father's journal, just a reference that said, 'my new weapon idea'. That was it, no details … not even what it did. I turned the entire house upside down and could not find any other notes or plans. I even quizzed my mother, thinking she knew something. I knew he never discussed business with her, she was just a woman, but I could leave no stone unturned. Westminster would not even tell me what they knew, just rightly assumed I should know. I should have. There is not anything, I assure you. Truly. Please, Your Grace, beating and torturing me well gain you nothing," he pleaded.

Vincent pursed his lips, crossed his arms over his chest and tapped his fingers on his arms impatiently, while he contemplated. Finally he sighed. "Not allowing your mother to be properly looked after, vexes me. I mean, really! I heard Westminster had her whisked away from you and you had no idea. That was most intolerable. I have it on good authority that she is quite safe and will be returned unharmed. You will see that no one spreads any unkind rumors about her disappearance. One should always look after the fair sex, so … I think you need to have a lesson." He hesitated, looking thoughtful. "Yes, that would give me some satisfaction." He nodded. "Please, not too long, gentlemen, I really must be going." With that he walked out the door.

An hour later they were exiting Tremayne's property. Vincent waited until they were clearly out of sight, then he knocked on the roof for the coach to stop. "Davis, join us inside please." As soon as Davis was inside, they started off again. "Well gentlemen, report."

Riggs started, "Well, Tremayne keeps a tight rein on his staff in some ways, but not their mouths. His mother's maid has been staying in his house since her disappearance as he won't pay her for just sitting around at the Dower House, so she's working as a maid at his house and none too happy about it. She doesn't understand what happened, just that Lady Tremayne disappeared along with the trunk she had packed to go to London. Tremayne told the staff not to discuss it with anyone, but they was all bursting to tell someone. They don't get to town much to see other people. Apparently old man Tremayne kept a tighter rein on everyone including his wife, even locked his office and didn't even allow anyone to clean it if he wasn't there."

Davis added, "The day Her Ladyship disappeared, there was a lot of yelling, and throwing things, and breaking things by Tremayne, but no one knows what really set it off. And before you ask, he didn't hit his mother, just yelled at her."

"Good. Very well, I'm fairly satisfied there was nothing. I am waiting to hear from an associate in the colonies."

*****

It was some time later, when Wyn managed to pull himself up off the floor. He stumbled over to the wall on which there was a mirror so ladies waiting to be shown to dinner might admire themselves. Other than looking pale and in pain, he looked normal. They had managed to inflict damage only where it wouldn't show. He stumbled to the bell pull and rang it. His butler appeared rather quickly. "You rang, sir?"

"Where is my wife? Is everyone all right?"

The butler looked puzzled. "Lady Tremayne is in her private sitting room, Your Lordship. As far as I know everyone is quite fine. Is something wrong?"

"Yes, our guests have left. I was told you were all held hostage."

The butler laughed. "I guess one could call it that. His Grace had brought baskets of delectables from Fortnum and Masons as a thank you to the staff. His men were regaling us with stories from London and some of the delightful places they travel with His Grace. When you rang, Davis and Riggs said they would look after you and for us to enjoy ourselves. I hope you didn't mind and were well looked after, Your Lordship. I would think it was a treat for you to be attended to by His Grace's staff."

Wyn sighed, "Yes, everything is fine. That will be all." He thought to himself, *How can one argue with that? Pomeroy was right, no one would believe him.*

Chapter Seventeen: Retiring

A couple months later, he made his decision. Life had been full of indecision lately, but of one thing he was sure. He was ready to retire. Jacob did not want his job. He was ready to retire as well. Vincent shrugged, it was understandable, they were the same age. He had mulled over who would take his place. He had met with his benefactor at the Home Office last week. They were agreeable on his selection.

He had invited Will and Ben to join him on their private hideaway island. It was a good place to escape the world and discuss business. He asked Will into their little office. "I have decided it is time for me to retire. I really am getting to old for all this cloak and dagger stuff. I have discussed it with our benefactor and he is agreeable. Therefore, I think you are ready to take over."

Will was astonished. He really hadn't thought about Vincent retiring. He fumbled for words. "Are … are you not going to … ah … give command to one of your own men?"

Vincent gave a little laugh. "We are all quite ready to retire. Jamison is already retired. Riggs needs to, his health is not good, but he is loyal and will follow my lead. Davis will probably still be willing to help out, but he has a family now and has

Jamison's job of running my household. We are all too old for this fun and games. It needs younger blood. You have shown some good leadership qualities. Ben is a good partner for you, but he is a follower, not a leader. He would not be happy with the job. I think you will. I understand your hesitation, but just say yes and jump in. You will be fine."

Will took a deep breath. "Very well, Your Grace. If you feel that it what should be done. I will willingly do it. Thank you for your confidence."

"You should probably keep your base of operation in London. I believe you kept Jacob's rooms?"

"Yes, we did. You are right, that is the best place to work from."

He handed Will an envelope. "When you arrive in London, you will go and see Lord Simon Peters at the Home Office. He will be expecting you. The ship will be at your disposal. Just let me know when you need it. Get in a pickle, and I am available for advice and I am sure Jacob would not leave you stranded, but you can do this."

"Yes, Your Grace. I will not embarrass either of you."

They spent the next few days discussing details that Will would need to know. Finally he sent Will and Ben off to London. Once they were gone, he went sailing for a few days. He was not ready to go back to his empty house. After only a week, stormy weather sent him home in spite of his lack of desire to be there.

Chapter Eighteen: Delaney

He was spending a lot of time in his conservatory, watching the rain and contemplating his future. He knew what he wanted, but how did he get it? He needed a family, and not just his children. He needed a woman in his life again. Being around Reina had made him feel that very deeply, but where was he to meet one. London was not the answer. Even though he had involved himself with the Ton social life in London, he didn't really feel a part of it. It had been part of the business venture. He didn't relish putting himself on the market during the season. When he had wandered through that chaos before, he hadn't seen any of interest. They were all after his title. All those scheming mamas trying to get a duke for their daughters. To them he was a ripe plum ready for the picking. He didn't want a debutant. He wanted someone near to his age, a lover, a companion. There had to be a better way. That would take a bit more effort.

Finally after three depressing days the rain stopped. Early the next morning he went for a brisk ride. That was what he needed, he needed to be outside. He was not used to being trapped indoors so long. After he returned, he headed for the orchard. He always went there after a mission, to relax and talk to Andrea, but this time it had been too wet. It was their place. The place that had created their meeting. He smiled remembering. Her little sister, Delaney had climbed the tree to get apples and got stuck. He had been home on summer break from Eton and had gone riding and found her, rescued her and had taken her home. That was when he had met Andrea. It had been love at first sight. The tree had become theirs, their meeting place when out riding, their haven to escape the cares of the world. When he had inherited the house, he built a bench around the tree as a place for them to sit.

Today as he approached the orchard, he could hear someone calling for help. He rushed forward, only to find someone in their special tree. "What are you doing up there?" he demanded angrily.

"Can we discuss that after you get me down," called a woman's voice. "This tree seems entangled in my hair and I can't get undone. I've been here ever so long and am quite exhausted."

He approached the tree cautiously, as one in his occupation always did. One never knew who one's enemies were, just because it was a woman did not mean she was not an enemy. Her horse was tied to a leg of the bench and her black riding hat was sitting on the bench. He looked up into the tree. She hadn't gotten very far, but she did look quite trapped. He could not see her face as her back was toward him, but he knew who it was. He had heard that she was home. He smiled and nodded and

116

decided to play ignorant. "Don't move, I'll have to come up," he said in a frustrated tone.

"I have not moved in ages. I am almost numb."

Vincent quickly stepped up on the bench and easily into the tree. A couple more limbs up and he was right behind her. He assessed the situation. He reached into his boot and pulled his boot knife. "Hold still, I have to use my knife to set you free."

"Oh, please do not cut my hair!" she wailed.

"I am pretty sure I can just cut the few small twigs that seem to have you held captive, but I am distressed to have to damage the tree." Her auburn hair was pulled up into a very fancy twist and the leafy little twigs were quite embedded in it. As he cut away at the entangled twigs, he took the time to quickly access her. She was nicely built, probably about five foot two, shapely, and well dressed in a black riding habit, slightly out of fashion. Her auburn hair was getting a few highlights of gray.

"Please do not tell His Grace about this. He will be very angry that I have been climbing his tree again."

"Again? So as a grown woman tis your habit to go about climbing trees?"

"Well, I was but a child the first time."

"A child?"

117

"So, am I free?"

He cleared his throat. "Not quite, almost." It took him several minutes to set her free as he was very careful not to cut her hair or damage the tree too much. Finally, he said, "All done, can you climb down on your own?"

"No, I do not think so. I am not sure I can move safely. I would probably fall and break my neck, which would serve me right for being so silly."

"Very well. You are not going to get upset that I am going to have to hold onto you, are you? I know it is most inappropriate, but we do what we must."

"No, I promise, as long as it is what you must do, I will not hold it against you."

"Back down very carefully. I will step down a limb at a time and then assist you. It is only three limbs." He placed an arm supportively around her waist, and thus they slowly descended the tree to the bench. At that point, she turned to give him her hand to step down to the ground. She gasped, "Vincent! It's you. I mean, I am sorry, Your Grace," quickly bobbing a curtsy and almost falling.

Vincent was having a hard time keeping a serious face. He wanted to laugh at her, she seemed quite flustered that it was he who had rescued her. He took the time to appraise her from the front. He hadn't seen her since his own wedding. He and

Andrea did not live close to her family, and he was at sea when Delaney had married and left for the Colonies.

None of Andrea's siblings looked alike. Andrea had been a tall blonde with very blue eyes and with a slender figure. Bertrand had been tall and slight as well, but with dark brown hair and eyes. Collin, the new Lord of the manor, was of average height with a bulky build, with blondish hair and green eyes. Delaney it seemed was of a buxom build, with green eyes and her fiery red hair had tamed to a more demure auburn with age.

"Your Grace, tis me, Delaney."

Vincent quickly pulled himself together, reached out and lifted her to the ground. "I know, but you still startled me. You do not have to call me 'Your Grace' you know. You are family. You should probably sit for a bit." He held her hand until she sat.

"I have been away from England too long. I shall have to re-learn proper English manners again."

Vincent laughed as he sat down beside her.

"It was terribly silly of me. I arrived back in England a few months ago. Stayed in London with friends for a short while, but just was not into London society. I have been home several weeks, but you have been gone. Not sure why I rode this way this morning, but when I saw the orchard I just had to see if I could still climb a tree. This one was the easiest with the bench. It's the one, is it not?"

He nodded. "I will be gracious enough not to say how long ago it was when I first pulled you out of this tree," he said smiling.

"I was ten and you were eighteen, home on break from Eton. You took me home in disgrace and met my sister."

He smiled remembering, "Yes, it was love at first sight. After that there was no one else for me but Andrea."

She laughed. "And quite jealous I was too. I had seen you first, and she stole you. I did not think it was fair."

"I heard you were back in England."

"How did you know?"

"I know Sir Charles Stafford. I saw him in London. He told me they had brought you home with them. I am sorry to hear about George," he replied.

"Thank you. Charles told me of your acquaintance. When George died last year, I stayed in Virginia. It was home for so many years. However, as our son died of influenza and George would never let a daughter inherit, the property went to a nephew. He finally came a few months ago and decided to sell the property. My brother had been wanting me to come home, we were all quite close if you remember. So when I told the Staffords I was going to return home, they told me they were moving back to England and could offer me escort. I was quite relieved."

"I am glad you had safe escort."

"Caroline wanted me to stay with them in London for awhile and go shopping. I should have as my wardrobe is so sadly out of fashion and I am out of mourning now, but I was just not ready to deal with London society yet, and then Collin was whining for me to come home and run his household."

"I understand. Andrea and I preferred it here. However, I recently helped a friend through such an arduous task. I would be delighted to offer my services as escort to you."

"A lady friend?" she asked, raising an eyebrow.

"She was a friend."

"I might just take you up on that offer, and with Alice Stafford's wedding soon, I need clothes. Collin has no desire to go to London. He says his brotherly duty to me does not include London."

Vincent chuckled, "Cannot say as I blame him for that, but I am wise to the ways of London and would be glad to be your escort. I know all the best places to shop."

They sat and chatted for about half an hour, then he offered to escort her home. "You should not have been out without an escort. If you had one, help would have been more quickly obtained," he teased. "I think I should take you to my house first and let Mrs. Greer put you to rights. Collin would shoot me if I let you return as you are. You still have twigs in your hair."

"Greer is still with you?"

"Yes, I had not the heart to let her go. She is quite deft with a needle and thread, and we have plenty to keep her busy."

"I believe I will take you up on that kind offer. I am having to train a new maid as my previous one would not leave Virginia. Barnes is doing well, but she is not as good as Greer. Besides, I would love to see her. Not many familiar faces about now days."

He laughed. "Very well." She picked up her hat and he untied her horse and they walked backed to the house.

Chapter Nineteen: London

A week later, Vincent was up and dressed. Delaney was staying with the Stafford's while in London. They had come down early for Charles' daughter Alice's wedding which was the day before Michaelmas. Charles thought he was insane to volunteer for such a chore, but he really had enjoyed shopping with Reina and having his input into her selections. He definitely was going to take pleasure in doing so with Delaney. They had already spent a fair amount of time together and he found her company most entertaining.

He arrived promptly at nine and was shown to the garden. Charles rose from the little table where he was having coffee and extended his hand. "Vincent, you are right on time as usual. And as usual the ladies are not. Would you like some coffee?"

"Yes, that would be very nice," he responded as he took the indicated chair across from Charles. "It is a lovely morning and your garden is splendid."

"Margaret, my sister-in-law loved her garden and managed it herself. Caroline has been adding her own touch since we have been here."

"How much longer will you stay in London."

"We are leaving as soon as the wedding is over. Only stayed in London to give Alice a season. She was thankfully engaged before it was over. She and her husband are going to stay in this house after their honeymoon, until my niece Alicia has a need for it, but I doubt that will happen. She and her husband are quite happy on their island. I saw no reason for Alice and Thomas to get another. We will spend very little time here, only when I need to take care of business. It is good to have someone in the house and it not sitting empty. Caroline and I will be most happy staying in Alicia's country estate. I can manage her affairs from there. What are you up to these days?"

"I am retired. Just ruminating in the country. Delaney and I crossed paths and I offered to bring her down early for the wedding so she could get new clothes. Come good sailing weather, I will go to India to see Alistair's family. Unless plans change, they will come back with me to put young Vincent at Eton."

"That will keep you occupied with young ones about again."

At that moment the ladies came through the doorway. The gentlemen immediately rose. Charles said, "My goodness, don't the three of you look lovely. I do not see why you need more clothes. You look stunning in the ones you have." He laughed at his own joke.

"Do not be ridiculous, Charles, women never have enough clothes," laughed Vincent. "Well ladies, I am ready if you are."

Charles promised to meet them at One O'clock for luncheon at Twinings. He hoped to rescue Vincent at that point and let the ladies shop on their own. However, he was unsure of Vincent's attachment to Delaney. Was he merely being kind to Delaney, were they just friends, or was he lonely and there more to it than that? Time would tell.

The first stop on their day's adventures was of course, Madame Devy's. Charles' wife, Caroline, and daughter, Alice had already done a fair bit of updating their wardrobes upon their arrival in London. Plus, they had already done shopping for the wedding, but were excited to help Delaney make her choices and then they all needed new accessories. After Delaney was measured, they spent the morning looking at designs and materials. Vincent sat in a comfortable chair and freely gave his approval or disapproval. He was surprised that Delaney listened to his suggestions.

"I love these blues and greens, but the yellow is just not for me," Delaney declared as she held up a section from a bolt of a dark yellow satin. "It makes my complexion look sallow," she complained frowning.

"Not the right shade," he said. He got up and starting looking through the swatches. He found a silk he liked, a sunny looking bright color. "Madame, do you have this material in stock?"

"Oui, Your Grace, I do." She sent one of her girls to the stock room. She soon returned with a roll of material.

Vincent took it and beckoned for Delaney to come to the large mirror. "If I may?" he asked as he draped the material around her. She was delighted with the look of the material on her.

"It is lovely."

"I told you to trust me." He removed the material from Delaney and handed it back to the girl. He went over to the design sketches and looked through them. He chose one and handed it to Madame. "That one, my treat."

Madame gave him a deep curtsy. "Oui, Your Grace, with pleasure."

They had been so enthralled with this task that Vincent sent a note to Charles, telling him they would come get him at his Club when they were ready for luncheon. Vincent was glad he had decided to do that as it was slightly after two when they arrived to get Charles. After a delightful and very noisy luncheon, after all, the ladies had to tell Charles all about their morning, Charles was gratefully returned to peace and quiet at his club; and Vincent took the ladies to Grisham's for shoes, then several places for parasols and hats and reticules. It was an exhausting day for the ladies, so it was decided that there would be no evening excursions. Besides a couple new gowns for Delaney would be delivered tomorrow, so they would plan an evening out for then.

Vincent and Delaney spent almost a month in London while Delaney shopped. If they hadn't been up too late at the opera or some party, they usually went riding in the early morning in the park. Then after changing, they would go shopping and end up somewhere for tea.

One day on an outing they passed the Crooked House. "Oh my goodness!" cried Delaney. "Is that thing still standing? I remember seeing it as a child."

"It has been standing since 1687. They used improper materials and it has been leaning precariously for years. It was a meat market and had a secret passage to deliver meat directly to the Windsor Castle kitchen. Rumor has it that Charles II used it to meet with mistress Nell Gwyn."

She looked at him askance. "Oh, you are teasing. I never heard that."

He chuckled. "As a child, I am sure you would not have been told such a thing."

The day before the wedding, Vincent was invited to the Stafford's for dinner. He could tell when he arrived that Delaney seemed distressed but was trying hard not to show it. The house was full of guests from out of town for the wedding, so it was not until after dinner that they were free to escape to the garden for a moment of quiet.

"Are you going to tell me what has you upset?" he asked as they walked around in the garden.

"What makes you think I am upset? It is just all these people and the excitement of the wedding."

"No, it is not just that. I am very good at reading people. Something has upset you. Maybe I can help."

"I received a letter today from George's Goddaughter. He became her Godfather a couple years before we were married. You remember that George was thirty-two when we married. Michaela is fifteen years younger than me. We have kept in touch. Apparently my letter telling her I was coming home had not reached her when she mailed this one. So it went to Virginia, then to Collin's and finally here. She asked me what to do? They are in terrible trouble. I do not know what to tell her."

"Where are they?"

"They live in Ireland, near the sea between Waterford and Cork. They had such a lovely estate, but the bad weather, the famine, and the political situation has nearly ruined them. They have had such a hard time the last few years. Her mother, sister-in-law, and her husband died of illness during that time. She had to move home. She has no children of her own. She and her younger brother, Sean, both live at home and help their father." She gave a little giggle, "They are Irish twins, only eleven months apart." She grew teary, "With a little help from us, they managed to keep the taxes paid, and now there is an awful man trying to run them off their land. What can I do?"

"Nothing this evening nor tomorrow as we have obligations to our friends. We shall deal with it after that. Just trust me."

"Oh Vincent, you are a darling, but what can you do? You are a dear to offer, but …"

"Trust me. Now let us go back to the party and enjoy being with our friends." He steered her back into the house.

By two o'clock the next day, the wedding was over, the wedding breakfast had concluded, the guests had left, and the servants were quite busy cleaning up after it all. Charles, Caroline, Delaney and Vincent sat in the Drawing Room having a quiet drink. The men were laid back in their chairs, Brandy in hand, eyes closed. The ladies were sitting sipping their Sherry.

Caroline sighed. "I am done with London. I am ready to retire to the country. I do not think I will do anything for at least a week."

"I know you better than that. How long will it take you to pack, my dear?" asked Charles.

"Not long. I have been packing things that we were not going to be using, so all that we have left to pack are the few things we have needed the last few days. I am sure our very efficient servants will have it done post haste. We should be able to leave tomorrow." She smiled at her husband.

"You are the most efficient of women." He reached over and took her hand and brought it to his lips and kissed it.

Delaney sighed and closed her eyes. "I am finished shopping. I am done with London as well. I am ready to go home."

Vincent did not even bother to open his eyes. "No, you are not. You want to go to Ireland."

She sighed. "True, but that will take some time to organize."

He chuckled. "Already done. My ship stands ready to sail. How long will you take to pack? All you have to do is sort out what to take to Ireland and the rest will go home."

She stared at him a moment, stunned. "Really?" Vincent nodded. "Well, I am not some silly goose. I, too, am very efficient. I have been packing away the things I have purchased. All that was left was for today, so Barnes should be able to have me ready to leave tomorrow as well."

He laughed. "That comes from a woman who got stuck climbing a tree."

Charles laughed, but said, "I heard that story. She was but a child though."

It was Vincent's turn to laugh. "No, it was just last month."

Charles roared with laughter. Caroline looked at Delaney and said, "Really Delaney?"

Delaney huffed, "I refuse to discuss it."

Vincent finished off his drink and stood. "Well then, I shall take my leave and see you first thing in the morning. Charles, Caroline, it was a beautiful wedding. Thank you for letting me be here to witness it." With that he exited the room and the house.

Delaney waited until she heard the front door close, then she shot to her feet. "If you will excuse me, I need to find Barnes and get my things together. They are a mess. I have not done anything. It will take me all night to get ready." With that she rushed out of the room.

Charles roared with laughter again. "I was not sure if there was something going on between them, but they definitely act like siblings. They may be in-laws but little sister can not let big brother get the best of her."

Chapter Twenty: Ireland

He arrived at the Stafford's very early the next morning, the sky was growing lighter, but the sun was not yet up. He had two large closed traveling coaches and two wagons and four outriders. The wagons were already mostly full of items as he was closing down the London house. The Stafford house was already a beehive of activity. Two large wagons were being loaded at the back door with their things, and their carriage and outriders were being prepared to leave as soon as they were ready. Delaney's trunks, bags and boxes were being carried down the stairs and placed in the foyer.

Vincent walked into the house as Delaney was coming down the stairs. He told her, "All your luggage that is going home goes on the first wagon. That which is going with us is going on the last wagon. Are you taking Barnes with you?"

"Yes, please."

"Then she rides in the last coach with us and Riggs. The other coach is the rest of my staff who will see our other things home. I hope you are ready for a sea voyage."

"Sounds exciting."

An hour later, the entourage headed for home was away. He and Riggs were settling Delaney and Barnes into their coach. It was a very cool morning, so they had placed heated bricks at their feet and gave the ladies blankets, then settled in themselves.

The next afternoon found them moored in the bay near Abbeyville, Ireland. Will and Ben had quietly boarded the ship before it left London. Keeping an eye on Ireland was always on their list of things to do. After they anchored, Will and Ben went ashore to get transportation for Vincent and to see what they could learn. Delaney was anxious to go ashore, but Vincent was very firm that they needed to learn what they could before visiting her friends.

Early the next morning, a carriage arrived on a small dock and their small boat rowed back to the ship. Will and Ben met with Vincent in his cabin. "The Dohertys are keeping themselves to themselves," reported Will. "They are pretty much secluded on their land. Being Catholic in Ireland is not easy right now. Plus this Josiah Quinn is trying to push them off their land. Rumor has it that he has been trying to marry Michaela, but she will have none of him."

Ben added, "Her brother, Sean was injured in a riding accident, though some donna think it was accidental. Some say he was forced off the road and down that embankment by Quinn. No one has seen any of them since. Everyone in the area seems afraid of Quinn, took awhile to find some who would even talk of him, in the tavern of course. I still have a hell of a head from all I had to drink last night, but we got some information on him. People think he has killed their stock and ruined some crops to run people off their land."

"Not that the very cold winter and the famine the last couple years had not already done that," interrupted Will.

"Thank you. At least I have an idea of what I am walking into. The letter to Delaney mentioned some of that, but tis good to have it confirmed."

"You are not going alone, are you?" said Will concerned.

"For the moment, yes. I shall have Riggs, and you and the crew will stand at the ready if I need you. After we go ashore, I want you to move the ship a little further out from the shore. Stay in the shelter of the bay, but keep a good watch."

"Aye, aye, Captain," chuckled Will.

Two hours later, they were arriving at the Doherty house. It was a beautiful piece of property, and was fairly well maintained, but one could tell it was starting to fall into decline. Delaney insisted on approaching the door herself when she saw the black wreath on the door. Vincent followed her up the steps onto the large porch. He knocked on the door. The butler opened the door, obviously an old family retainer as he looked them up and down before he said, "The family is not receiving visitors at this time."

Delaney held out her card, as well as the one she had received from Vincent. "Mrs. George Monahan, and His Grace, the Duke of Edgingham to see the family."

"Mrs. George, I remember Mr. George. It has been a long time. Please, come in. You can wait in the Drawing Room and I will see if someone can see you." He smiled and waved them in and led them to the Drawing Room. "My name is Tomas. I may be a few minutes."

"Thank you," replied Delaney smiling.

It was perhaps half an hour later when a slender, fragile looking gentleman in his thirties entered the room. He was about 5'7" tall, very thin and pale. He had piercing blue eyes and his hair was a dark blonde, a little longer than shoulder length, pulled back in a queue. His voice was very soft, and he did not sound well. "Mrs. Monahan, I am very surprised to see you. We received your letter about a month ago saying that you were returning home."

"You must be Sean. Oh, my goodness," she said, rising. "I did not receive Michaela's letter till a few days ago. This is my friend, His Grace, the Duke of Edgingham. He brought me to see you, to see if we could help in any way. How is your father? Michaela? How are you?"

"I should have written you. You have been so kind and generous to us. I know I should have told you, but I just could not face doing it yet. Michaela … Michaela died a couple weeks ago."

Delaney gasped and rushed to him intending to hug him, but he took both her hands in his and held them tightly. "She had too much to bear, looking after me, taking care of Father, worry about the farm. My accident caused Father to have a heart attack, it all was just too much for her."

Delaney started drawing him to the sofa and pulled him down to sit beside her. Vincent stood watching them intently. The poor man was quite overcome with grief. Before he could say anything, the door opened and the butler entered carrying a tray with a pitcher and glasses. "I thought some lemonade might be in order," he said, setting it on the low table by the sofa.

"Thank you, Tomas," replied Sean. "That will be all for now. I am sure we can serve ourselves."

Tomas nodded and left.

Vincent moved to the table and poured a glass of lemonade and took a sip. "I am most willing to help you, but you must be honest with us … Michaela."

She and Delaney had identical stunned looks on their faces. Michaela mumbled, "I … a … I …"

"Please do not insult my intelligence by denying it. It was an understandable thing to do when you were struggling on your own, but you are no longer alone. I must have the truth or I can do nothing to help you."

"How did you know?" she asked in almost a whisper. She let go of Delaney's hands, covered her face and burst into tears. "If I can not fool you who have never seen me, how will I ever fool him?"

"There is no need to do so. Tell us what he has done and what he has threatened to do."

Delaney poured lemonade for them both. "Vincent, how did you know? I would never have guessed."

"You do not look at ladies in the same way I do. There are many tell-tale signs if you know what to look for. She has no Adam's apple. She obviously does not shave, and women are just not shaped like men, front or back. It is very difficult to hide. Now, the truth, please."

"Josiah Quinn arrived last year after our horribly cold winters, the famine, so many people died, those who survived were starving. He started buying up their land and not paying all that much for it. If people resisted, he made sure what crops they had were damaged and stock was destroyed.

138

He left us alone while he picked on others. I had seen him in town a few times and he had tried to talk to me. Father or Sean was always with me, so protected me. About a month ago, I was at the Milliners selling her back some hats to make a little money, he tried to get friendly. Told me he wanted our land and he would find a way to take it. Told me I should marry him, that way my family could keep our home. I tried to ignore him, but he was very insistent. Sean arrived and it got ugly. Would have been a fight right then, but some other people arrived, so he left. His parting words were that we would be sorry." She burst into tears again.

This time Delaney slid closer and put her arms around her and held her. She managed to calm the woman down. "That was the day before he ran Sean off the road with his carriage. We had to put down the poor horse. Sean was very badly injured and died a couple days later. It was too much for Father, he had a heart attack. The doctor says there is nothing more he can do. He has left medicine to make Father comfortable but says he will not last long. He has been a family friend for years. It was his suggestion that I pretend to be Sean. We would say that I died, then after Father dies, I should leave the country, go somewhere safe. I do not know what to do. Quinn sent word on Monday that he would be here in a week's time. He would take what he wanted."

Delaney said, "That's two more days. We can be gone by then. You must certainly come home with me. You will be safe there."

"Running away is never the answer," replied Vincent. "We cannot move her father. I need to think. I am going for a walk. I suggest you both go rest and then dress appropriately for dinner." He walked to the bell pull and rang it.

Tomas entered within a few minutes. "Please send Barnes to the ladies. They need her attention. Is Riggs in the kitchen?" asked Vincent.

"Yes, Your Grace."

Vincent nodded. "Then take me to him." Tomas raised an eyebrow. Vincent smiled. "I know tis not proper, but right now propriety will not solve our problems."

Tomas nodded and led the way. As Vincent walked into the kitchen, Molly stood and looked quite shocked. Riggs had also stood, but did not look at all surprised. Vincent looked at him and said, "Well?"

"The house is in a sad state, Your Grace. These are the only servants left. The bad crops the last couple years have left the family in trouble, could not pay the staff, food is a little scarce as well. Good thing they have a decent kitchen garden, but that is about all. This Quinn is quite a troublemaker."

"I'd like to get me hands on him meself. Bash him with ma' skillet, I would," grumbled Molly.

Vincent smiled. "One never knows. You might get that opportunity. See here, I know your household is in trouble, we are here to help." He pulled his wallet from his breast pocket and pulled several notes from it. "I want you to go to town and buy what you need for meals. Also, I need you to get the staff back or hire more. I will assure back pay will be made and they will receive a month in advance."

The old couple looked at each other. Tomas said hesitantly, "I do not think the Squire and Mr. Sean would like that. Their pride you know."

"I know about Mr. Sean and Miss Michaela, Tomas. She is allowing me to be in charge. Just please do what I ask. And Molly I suggest a nice beef broth, roast chicken and vegetables and scones for dinner. People who have not eaten well for awhile, should not feast on heavy food, no sauces. Keep the helpings small, no one should have too much for a few days."

Molly looked askance at him. "And what would Your Grace know of starvation?"

He smiled. "I was a ship's Captain once upon a time. I know what it is to run out of rations. I have seen starving sailors gorge themselves when food was available, then be very sick after, sometimes even die. Not something your family needs. Trust me, we shall get them through this, but we need to work together."

"Your Grace, the shops will not sell to us," remarked Tomas. "They are afraid of Quinn and his hooligans. If they sell to Catholics, he will do damage to their stores. We have to fend for ourselves."

"Very well, Riggs, go get our carriage. We are going to town shopping."

Chapter Twenty-One: A Solution

On the way into town, Vincent explained his plan to Riggs. "You can drop me in town, then go signal the ship. I need you to bring back Ben with a half dozen sturdy lads. Be sure they are well armed. They should be prepared to stay a few days as we have no idea how this will all play out. Bring back the cash box and several extra pistols. Will needs to stay with the ship to protect it and be prepared for anything. We do not know if we might need more help. I hope we can handle this quickly, but who knows. Then trade this carriage for a large wagon."

"As you wish, Your Grace. Where do you want me to meet you?"

As they drove into the town, he scanned the main street. "Leave me at the Green Grocer's. When you come back, pick up the orders there, at the Butcher's and the General Store. They will all be told the orders are for the ship. I will wait for you at that little tea shop over there when you are done."

"Very good, Your Grace. I will see you shortly."

At the Green Grocers, he placed his order and told the man his wagon would be picking up the supplies for his ship. Then he walked to the

Butcher's and placed a large order and told them the same thing. Finally he stopped at the General Store and placed his final order. Then he went to the tea shop, had tea and biscuits and waited. It was a little over an hour later that the wagon arrived. He could see the street well from the window by his table. He waited until they had picked up all the orders. Then he picked up his little package, left the shop and joined them at the General Store. As he climbed aboard the wagon and it started forward, the owner who was dusting the boxes in front of his store, waved at him and called, "Your Grace, you're going the wrong direction. Your ship is back that way."

Vincent tipped his hat and replied, "Thank you for your assistance. Yes, it is, but I am not going that way."

By the time they arrived back at the house and pulled up to the kitchen door, two footmen came out to help them. Vincent climbed down from the wagon being careful with his special package and walked into the kitchen. Molly was positively glowing as she ordered people about, telling them where to put things. He walked over, handed her the package and said, "Something special for you and Tomas to have with your tea. A thank you for staying with Michaela." He gave her a kiss on the cheek and walked on into the house. She carefully opened the package and found a box of fancy treats from the tea shop. "Bless his heart, what a nice young man."

The ladies were still in their rooms, so he took the time to walk about the house and grounds, talk to Ben, and do his planning. Tomas brought him a message that Squire Doherty was awake and would like to see him. By the time he needed to dress for dinner, he was ready. He brought Riggs up on his plans and went down to the Drawing room to wait for the ladies.

When they arrived, he was quite bowled over at the beauty who accompanied Delaney. Michaela looked quite stunning in a simple black silk evening dress, with her hair done in a simple updo. She only wore plain silver ear studs and no other jewelry. He assumed any jewels she owned had been sold to keep the household running. "You ladies both look quite lovely this evening."

They both thanked him. Michaela remarked, "I hope you do not mind simple fare for dinner. We live a farmer's life here."

"I enjoy simpler fare myself. Rich foods are not good for one, even though we enjoy them immensely." He smiled.

Tomas announced dinner a few minutes later. When a footman served the first course of a small bowl of beef broth, Michaela looked at Tomas, who was standing in the doorway, in surprise. He nodded toward Vincent and gave a slight shrug of his shoulders. The main course of roast chicken and vegetables brought tears to her eyes. Vincent and

Delaney were trying hard to keep the conversation light and witty over the meal. When the final course of syllabub was served, she could no longer be silent on the subject. "Your Grace, I am quite sure I have you to thank for this lovely dinner."

"It is nothing. It is not only my pleasure, but my duty. Let us finish our dessert and withdraw to the Drawing Room, we have much to discuss." Thirty minutes later had the ladies seated in the Drawing Room with coffee, and Vincent standing by the fireplace with a glass of Brandy.

After Tomas left them, Vincent said, "I had a lovely conversation with your father a little earlier this evening."

"Father? He saw you?" Michaela was quite startled.

"After some nourishing broth, a rest and some good news, he was feeling much better. I discussed my plans with him, and he is quite agreeable. Timing has been most excellent. He says Father Conor from The Friary will be bringing communion to the household tomorrow afternoon."

Michaela was very confused, but responded, "Yes, he has been bringing us communion since it is not wise for us to leave the house to go to Mass."

"Perfect." Vincent moved to sit on the settee with Michaela where he had purposely placed her and sat his glass on the table. He sat turned so he could face her. "The Squire explained the awful law that Catholics cannot leave their land to one heir. They must leave it divided equally to all male members of the family."

Delaney gasped. "That is terrible, the land would be divided into tiny pieces."

Michaela nodded. "Yes, and most would give in and sell."

Vincent continued, "Therefore, I have bought the land. As an English Noble, no one will question my ownership or what I do with it. Your family can continue on as you have, only with more success."

"Thank you, that is most kind."

"It is a part of the marriage contract, because unless you strongly object, your father has agreed that it is to everyone's best interest for you to marry me tomorrow."

Michaela for the moment was speechless. Vincent reached over and took her hand. "I am sorry that is not a very romantic proposal, but the situation requires immediate action. I promise you I will take good care of you and your father, but I am sure if you are not happy there will be enough things not handled properly enough that you can divorce me later and go on with whatever life you choose."

Michaela recovered herself enough to respond, "But Your Grace, there are many reasons that cannot happen."

"Unless you really hate the idea, I can think of none."

She took a deep breath and replied, "Number one, I am Catholic and you are not. Number two, I do not have any title and you are a Duke." Tears formed in her eyes, "And most importantly, number three, I cannot give you children. Donovan and I were married for eighteen years and I was unable to have any."

He smiled. "Number one, I do not care. Number two, I do not care, besides after you marry me, you will have a title. And most importantly, I do not require children. I have a son to inherit and he has two sons, so my family line will go on. I merely require a companion, a partner."

Delaney finally found her voice, "Do not be silly, Michaela, say yes. He is a wonderful man. You will be deliriously happy."

Vincent looked sad for a moment. "You have not mentioned a really big reason." Michaela looked at him questioningly. "I am old enough to be your father."

She laughed. "I am thirty-seven years old. We are both mature adults. I do not consider that a reason. I would be honored to be your wife, but I must tell you …"

Vincent cut her off, "Then we have nothing else to discuss. I am sure you ladies can handle everything from here. I will take care of the priest. You can do everything else." He brought her hand to his lips and kissed it. "Oh, that reminds me, I do not have a ring. We can use my signet ring," he held up his little finger with the signet ring, "until we can check the family jewels for something you like."

Delaney sighed, "Oh Vincent, you have never been to a Catholic wedding? Wedding rings have to be blessed. Do not worry, I will provide a ring for my Goddaughter."

"See, we are ready," remarked Vincent.

Michaela sighed, "But I really must say …"

Vincent interrupted again, "Unless you really want to say no, I think we all have plenty to do. I will leave you ladies to your plans. I have things to do to carry out mine, so you must excuse me." With that he kissed her hand again. He walked over and kissed Delaney on the cheek and left the room.

Chapter Twenty-Two: Sunday

Vincent was up very early the next morning. First on his itinerary was the kitchen. He found Molly baking bread and starting breakfast. "Molly, your dinner last night was perfect. Let us keep it simple for a couple more days, then you can cook to your heart's content. This morning the ladies will have breakfast in bed, and I shall be back in about half an hour for mine. Luncheon today will probably be late and since tomorrow may be a trying day, I think we should have an early light dinner rather than tea and retire early. Tomorrow we shall take as it comes."

She nodded. "Very sensible, Your Grace."

"Tomas, tomorrow please keep all the servants in the house until I tell you it is safe for them to do otherwise."

Tomas sighed, "As you wish, Your Grace, but I do know how to use a gun."

Vincent smiled. "I am sure you do. You and the lads can be prepared to defend the house if necessary, but my men are well trained and they should be enough to protect you all." He started to leave. "Oh and Molly, Father Conor may be joining us for luncheon."

"He usually does when he comes, Your Grace."

Vincent laughed and left the house through the kitchen door and went to find Ben. After giving him instructions, Vincent returned to the house for breakfast.

The ladies came down as he was eating and joined him at the table for coffee. Michaela was mostly silent while Delaney prattled on about her thoughts for the wedding. Finally Michaela said, "Vincent, I really must tell you something."

He looked at her and said, "Yes?"

"You said that later I could get a divorce if I want to. I must tell you that the Catholic Church will not allow that."

He sighed. "I find that if someone really wants something, there is always a way. Let us not worry about that now." He smiled at her. "Now if there is anything you ladies need, feel free to send Riggs to town to buy it." He finished his breakfast and left them alone.

Father Conor arrived about twelve and immediately went to see Squire Doherty. The Squire immediately sent for Vincent. The three of them were secluded for well over an hour. Michaela told Delaney, "See I told you. Father Conor will not marry us. We will just have to give in and go to England."

"I do not think you should underestimate Vincent. He is not a man who takes no for an answer. He always gets his way."

Michaela did not believe her. "Even if he does say yes, I still say we do not need any plans. It does not matter what I wear, and we do not need to do anything special. I am not ripping up my few precious flowers for decorations."

"I heartily agree. You ladies are decoration enough," said Vincent entering the room.

"He said 'yes'?" asked Michaela incredulously.

"Of course, we are not doing anything wrong. Just merely rushing the process. I got a very long lecture on religion, but in the end, we shall be married shortly."

"Oh my goodness!" cried Michaela. "I have to get ready." She rushed from the room.

"What did you have to do?" asked Delaney.

"His very poor parish is in desperate need of funds. All they have left after Cromwell, is a thatch-roofed building, they call the Mass-House. I offered help. As I said, it is not as though we are doing anything wrong."

An hour later, he was kissing his bride. Squire Doherty had insisted he was well enough that he was not missing his daughter's wedding and was carried downstairs in a chair by the footmen. He also decided he could join them for the lovely wedding luncheon of chicken, vegetables, soda bread, and even a small cake.

After Father Conor left and the Squire was settled back in his room, Delaney, Michaela and Vincent were sitting in the Drawing Room having tea. Delaney said, "I am exhausted. I am going to retire early and sleep late. After all I have eaten today, I do not require dinner. I shall see you all probably tomorrow afternoon." She kissed Michaela on the cheek and left the room.

Michaela gave Vincent a shy smile. "If you do not object, I too am rather tired."

Vincent rose and held out his hand and she stood. "Of course I do not object. Please get a good night's sleep. Feel free to sleep late as well, I can handle tomorrow." He intended to kiss her on the cheek, but she turned her head and he kissed her on the lips. He tried to control his desire for her, but it was not easy as she pressed herself into him. "Michaela, you do not have to do anything you do not want to do."

She gave him a flirtatious look and said, "Right now, I am going to bed." He swore she swayed her hips a bit as she walked out the door.

He rang for Tomas and the two of them went through the house being sure all doors and windows were locked for the night. He then went to his room, removed his coat, waistcoat, untucked his shirt, and was just sitting in a chair removing his boots, when he heard the communicating door to the adjoining room open. Michaela walked into the room wearing a very thin muslin nightgown that did nothing to hide her slender body. He stood. "I did not know that was your room."

"It is not, but since we were getting married, I moved there today." She was moving slowly across the room to him.

"Michaela, I told you that you do not have to do anything you do not want to do. I know I rushed you into this. You do not have to share my bed."

"Does that mean that you do not desire me?" She was standing quite close and he was having a hard time keeping his hands to himself.

"Dear God, yes. I do, but ..."

He didn't get to finish the sentence. She reached up her hand and caressed his cheek, then pulled his head toward her and pressed her lips to his. He groaned and pulled her into his arms and their kisses grew quite passionate.

Over an hour later, they lay in each other's arms. She had her head on his shoulder and was caressing his chest. "Vincent?"

"Yes, my love?"

154

"There really is something else you should know."

He rolled over on his side facing her, keep her in his embrace. "And what is that?"

"I know you said there is always a way, but according to my Church, once our marriage has been consummated, our marriage is valid and divorce in not allowed."

"Father Conor explained that all quite explicitly. I had very good intentions of not taking you to bed tonight. I still believe there is always a way and I wanted to give you good reasons if you wanted them, but I lost those good intentions when you walked through that door. I am sorry very sorry if I took away your out."

"I never said I wanted an out." She smiled at him.

He smiled back. "Good, I do not want one either." He pulled her back to him and kissed her passionately.

Chapter Twenty-Three: Quinn

The next morning, he was having coffee in the library while he looked over their book collection. Tomas knocked on the door, then entered. "Lookouts say they are coming. Ben says everything is ready in the garden."

Vincent nodded, handed Tomas his cup and left the house. He had left Michaela in bed and hoped she would stay there awhile. He went straight to where Ben had set up a table with several loaded pistols and a target set up at a goodly distance. He picked up the first pistol and fired at the target, hitting it slightly off center. "Sight is off a bit," he remarked to Ben. He picked up the next one and fired again. This one went dead center. After he fired the third one, he heard a voice moving closer from the front of the house say, "Looks like you missed."

Ben was standing near the target and replied, "No, he hit dead center, again. He always does. It went through the same hole as the last shot."

"Hmph," snorted Quinn. "Likely story. I am here to see the Squire."

Vincent picked up and fired the fourth pistol. He replied without looking at him. "The Squire is not well. He is not seeing anyone. You can talk to me." Again the bullet hit dead center.

"I ain't talking to you. You ain't nobody. I have business with the Squire."

Vincent turned to look at him. The man had two ruffians standing beside him. "You shall have to talk to me or get off my property."

Again the man snorted, "Ain't yer property."

"I bought it yesterday."

Quinn grew quite red in the face. "You what?"

At that moment Michaela exited the house carrying a mug of ale. She was smiling, but Vincent could tell she was terrified. Her left hand was clenched on her skirt and her right hand shook a little. He smiled at her.

Quinn leered at her. "Well if it tisn't the delicious Michaela bringing me a drink. Thank you, love."

Vincent picked up the next pistol and aimed it at Quinn. "You do not have her permission to use her Christian name, and if you ever speak thus to my wife again, I will shoot you where you stand."

Quinn sputtered, "Yer what?"

Michaela had reached her husband and set the mug on the table. Vincent wrapped his left arm around her waist and pulled her toward him. He bent his right elbow, placing the pistol on his shoulder and kissed her quite passionately. Then he turned to look at Quinn, not letting go of his wife. "I do not believe we have any business to discuss. Get off my property and out of this area entirely. No one wants you here. If you and your cronies are not completely gone by sunrise tomorrow, my men will see that you are, and they will not be gentle about it."

Quinn sputtered a moment or two more, then turned, took three steps, then turned back as he pulled a pistol from his belt.

Vincent ran his left hand up Michaela's back to her head, turning her face into his chest as he lowered his pistol and shot Quinn right between the eyes before his gun even cleared the belt. He stared at the other two. "Get that garbage off my property and remove yourselves and any of your friends from this area by tomorrow morning or my men will see that you do."

The men were frantically nodding their heads as they dragged Quinn to his horse and threw him over it. They quickly rode away.

Vincent released his wife, laid his pistol on the table, took a drink from the mug of ale and then turned to her. He smiled. "I think I need a nap. I did not get much sleep last night. Would you care to join me?"

She smiled, and nodded, and they walked toward the house hand in hand.

Epilogue

Ten months later, Vincent sat on the edge of the bed looking at his wife and newly born daughter. "I think that proves you are capable of having children."

Michaela smiled at him. "It is a miracle."

Vincent shook his head. "You know it is not always the woman's fault there are no children?"

She ignored the question. "Are you sure Alistair is not upset that you have another child?"

He laughed. "Alistair and his family may have only been back in England a month, but you know they love you. He is excited to have a baby sister to spoil and cannot wait until you feel up to visitors. Elizabeth is delighted as well. She says since she and Alistair seem only capable of having boys, she is thrilled to have a girl to shop for. She says boys' clothes are boring. She cannot wait to shop for girl things for Fiona."

She looked down at the baby sleeping in her arms. "Can I have another?" She looked up at him and gave him a dazzling smile. "Please."

He laughed. "I think I am a little old to be siring children."

She raised an eyebrow, looked down at the baby, then back up at him. "Apparently not."

He laughed again. He reached over and caressed the baby's cheek and kissed his wife. "Well, I certainly do not plan on being celibate, so we shall see. We shall see."

Made in the
USA
Lexington, KY